www.ChloeEmile.com

# The Fall River Family Saga

## CHLOE EMILE

This is a work of fiction. Names, characters, organizations,places, events, and incidents are either products of the author's imagination or are used fictitiously.

The Fall River Family Saga
Copyright © 2015 by Chloe Emile. All rights reserved.

No part of this book may be reproduced, or stored in a retrieval system, or transmitted in any form or by any means, electronic, mechanical, photocopying, recording, or otherwise, without express written permission of the author.

ISBN-13: 978-1987859133
ISBN-10: 1987859138

# CONTENTS

# CHAPTER ONE

The year was 1847. Ireland was losing her sons and daughters to the potato famine and typhus. Each day, families were leaving the country to find better lives—and to escape death. Without their main staple, the people, as well as the animals, were in perpetual danger.

After losing both his parents, nineteen-year-old Ryan Lochlan knew in his gut that he had to leave. To stay would mean being lonely. Besides, he had a dream that burned inside of him, and he vowed to make it a reality. With the help of his parish priest, he was able to secure passage on a ship to Liverpool and, from there, another ship to America.

During the lonely two-month journey, Ryan often wondered if he had made the right decision. Many of the others on board were emigrants like himself who had lost everything back home. To escape was the miracle they had been praying for. To many, the trip was the only dream they had left.

The ship docked in Boston's boisterous harbor. The ship's captain had chosen Boston for the large number of Irish there. Finding work would be easier for them.

On the afternoon he arrived, Ryan walked the busy docks and noticed many offering work there. Taking one of those jobs would've been easy, and he felt the universe had something better out there for him.

As he ventured away from the dock, the scent of the sea air seemed to fade as if it would soon be just a memory. He walked through the busy streets until he came upon a quieter part of town with stores and homes. The aroma of fresh-baked bread caught his attention, and for the first time since he'd left his native land, he felt homesick.

Ryan looked up and saw a sign that read O'Farrell's Pub. He felt it was a sign of hope, and he was right. He looked through the windows at the patrons happily eating and drinking inside.

After devouring two hearty bowls of stew at O'Farrell's, he went out to get a job with the Old Colony Railroad. He knew he had made the right move. The wages from the railroad were better than those on the dock, and they also provided lodging for their workers.

In a short time, Ryan was made foreman to his crew, and a young man about his age who'd come from Pennsylvania, Mick Dawson, was his second in command. The two became fast friends and did everything together. The only time they were not together was on payday. Mick would enjoy his free time in the local pubs, but Ryan liked going to a little restaurant called The Shamrock, a lovely little place owned by Nora and Paul Kelly, a middle-aged couple who served traditional Irish dishes and the best stew, as good as his mother's. The restaurant had a friendly atmosphere that reminded him of home.

On a quiet Sunday, Ryan decided to treat himself to lunch. He walked into The Shamrock and went to his usual seat in the back when Nora called out to him.

"Your usual, love?"

"You read me mind, Nora darlin'."

She made her way to the table with a cup of coffee. He had to admit that, even in her mid-fifties, Nora was still a fine-looking woman with golden-brown hair sprinkled throughout with just a touch of silver, and hazel eyes that seemed to glow amber.

Nora herself made no secret that Ryan was her favorite customer. Why, how could she not love that tall young man with hair the color of coal, eyes as blue as a glacier, and a smile that could melt the heart of any woman from eight to eighty-one? Paul had been a handsome man in his day, but that boy there, well... He was a prince that came only once in a woman's lifetime. She smiled at him.

"You know there's a fresh, hot blueberry pie back there with your name on it. I'll go get you a nice, healthy slice"

"Nora, you're gonna spoil me."

"Until some fine young lass comes along and steals you away."

"There could be no woman to take your place. No one could cook like you."

She laughed and headed back to the kitchen. She knew it true that one day, some fine one would catch his eye, and he'd vow his heart to her for all his days.

After Ryan worked four months in Boston, the Colony Railroad merged with the Fall River Line. At that time, half the Boston crew was to be sent south to Fall River, and Ryan was among them.

As the supply wagons and men left Boston, they left behind the towns too until only farmland lay before them. Passing by farm after farm, Ryan thought of home and his parents. Many of the men that worked with him were saving their money to bring their families over. How he wished his family were still alive and there with him. His parents would've loved this land.

He looked over at Mick. "Well, we'll be there soon. I'll have you handle the wagons while I find out from the head foreman where we bed down and let him know we're here."

"Why do I always get the glory work?" Mick mussed up his hair, which was the color of straw, and sighed.

"Because you love the glory. You live for this, that's why. Besides, I hear it drives women crazy."

As they both started to laugh, a shot rang out. Their smiles faded, and they jerked their heads toward the source of the noise ahead.

A man in his fifties was blocking the middle of the road and holding the shotgun.

"Now fellas, the way I sees it is you only got one way out, that being to turn them there wagons around and head back down the road, or we'll just say it won't be a good idea."

Ryan started to get off the wagon, but Mick tried to stop him, saying, "What do you think you're doing?"

"I'm gonna go talk to him."

"You do know he's got a shotgun, don't you?"

"Yeah, I see it, Mick. Don't worry. I don't think he'll really use it."

"Ryan, he'll blow a hole right through you."

"Well then, that's a bad thing for me, but it would mean you'll be the boss."

He winked at Mick, got off the wagon, and carefully took a few steps toward the old man, a friendly smile on his face.

"Good day to you, sir. My name is Ryan Lochlan, and I work with the railroad. We were told we have permission to use this road, from a Mr. Daniel McVinny."

The old man raised his shotgun and pointed it at Ryan's chest.

"That would be me. Now, young fella, you seem like a right fine young man, so I'm only gonna tell you this one more time. Now, mind you, I don't like repeating myself, so I would take it kindly if ya would take them there wagons back down the road."

Shrugging, Ryan took a few steps back and headed for the wagon. He climbed back on board.

"Well boss, what do we do?" Mick asked.

"Like the man says, we move them there wagons."

After taking a much longer route, the two men arrived at camp a little after sunset that evening. They were greeted by the head foreman, Miles Lafferty, a short, balding man in his late fifties with a pockmarked face and beady eyes. His teeth were stained brown from the foul cigars he smoked, and he smiled at them. Ryan wanted to shiver at the glimpse of Lafferty's teeth.

Lafferty wasn't sure of Ryan Lochlan. Something about Ryan made him wonder if he was a plant by the big brass in Boston, to find out what was going on in Fall River. He'd been hearing a lot of talk from the drivers that the brass was noticing that the numbers didn't match. His next thought was maybe he should let a few shipments stay intact, just to let the talk die down.

"Well, it took you long enough," Lafferty said.

Ryan got off the wagon. "We were stopped on the road by an older man and his very unfriendly shotgun."

"That would be Daniel McVinny."

"Am I to understand that you know this person? Why wasn't he mentioned in any of the reports?"

"Oh sure, he's the owner of the road down there. He really is just set in his ways. Most of the time, we take the other route and don't even use his road."

Ryan looked confused, slowly shaking his head.

Lafferty sighed and tried to explain. "About six months ago, the railroad made an agreement with McVinny to pay him four thousand dollars for the use of his road, to bring our supplies in. Well, it seems the old man agreed, took the money, and then turned back on the agreement. He stops every wagon that comes to his road."

"You mean you paid this man four thousand dollars and still don't use the road?"

"That's right."

"Why don't you ask for the money back?"

"Well, you see, the brass in Boston don't know about this."

"And the reason for this is…?" Ryan couldn't believe or comprehend what he was hearing. "Boston doesn't know about this because—and I'm guessing on this—if they knew, it wouldn't look good on your part."

Lafferty crossed his arms. He wasn't doing too well in their debate. "Are you trying to say I had something to do with all this?"

"I'm not saying that at all. But if you know anything about it, it would be wise to say something now. I just want to know: was the money sent by courier from Boston?"

"The money was sent with a supply wagon, and from there, I had two men take it to McVinny."

"You said the money was sent by supply wagon. Did McVinny let them go before he got the money? I mean, if he let the wagons pass before the agreement, why did an agreement need to be made? Were these men trustworthy?"

"I believed they were."

"You believed they were? How did you get to be foreman? Are they still around? I'd like to talk to them."

"I don't know where they are right now, but I'll find them."

Ryan looked at him with the suspicion that something about his story still didn't sound right. "Tell ya what I'm gonna do. I'm going back to the McVinny farm in the morning and talk to the man. When I get back, I'll speak to those two men."

"Be my guest. Oh, by the way, what would you like on your tombstone? You know old man McVinny ain't gonna let you off his property alive."

"I don't think I'll need a tombstone just yet." He left Lafferty and headed to the stables.

Halfway there, Mick ran into him. "Hey, Ryan, look, we got real cabins, and our names are on the door. We have real beds. Real beds, Ryan, not cots!"

"Mick, I'm gonna need you to take care of the crew tomorrow. I have to go to the McVinny farm in the morning."

"Have you lost your mind? The old man with the shotgun is a bit touched in the head. Now that I think about it, you might be too, for wanting to go back there."

"I don't know, but it seems funny that a man takes four thousand dollars and then goes back on an agreement and doesn't give the money back. I don't know how crazy he is. Maybe he would give the money back."

Ryan shook his head at the mystery of it all.

At sunup, he came out of the stable with his horse. As he mounted, he said, "Mick, you keep the crew moving, and I'll get back as soon as I can."

"Hey, what if you don't get back?"

"Then you're the new foreman."

He smiled and rode off.

# CHAPTER TWO

Breakfast at the McVinny home was a bit more refined than what Ryan and Mick were used to. It was a family event. Molly Payton McVinny was Daniel's lovely wife. Her hair was auburn, and she had hazel eyes that would change to amber when she smiled. She had been raised at a mission school and worked as a teacher in Pennsylvania when she first met Daniel. She thought him a striking man, with his blond hair and piercing blue eyes. He had to be well over six feet four. As both would say, they fell in love at first sight and were married a year later.

Daniel brought her to Fall River, where they bought the farm, worked on it together, and made it the finest farm in the land. Two years after they married, their first girl, Abigail McVinny, was born.

Abby was a lovely girl with hair the color of chestnuts and eyes of emerald green. Two years after came Jennifer Katherine, whose dark-brown hair and blue eyes gave an Irish look to the girl.

After a period of five years, Molly had two more girls, fraternal twins named Annie and Mary. They both had their father's blond hair, but their eyes were a soft velvet brown. Because Annie was the smaller of the two, she was always called Little Annie. Molly taught her girls as if they were at school, and unlike other girls their age in the village, they could read and write at an early age. Molly also taught them how to cook and sew. From Daniel, the girls learned how to help out on the farm.

As they all sat at the breakfast table, Abby, then a sassy twenty-year-old, thought it a good time to raise a subject she'd been curious about.

"Papa, what was the reason the wagons couldn't go through today?"

Molly looked up from her plate. "Daniel, what have you done again? Didn't we discuss this last month? You gave me your promise.

Daniel, you always said your word was your bond. Was that a lie?"

He put down his piece of bread. "Now, Molly, don't you be a-judging me 'fore you hear what I has to say. After all, you had seen them there railroad fellas, all of 'em in the wagon. It just doesn't seem right."

At the mention of fellas, all four girls' heads looked up from their plates.

"Fellas? How many fellas, Papa?" was Jenny's question. She was nineteen and keen on meeting a fella.

Daniel was ready to answer when Little Annie asked a question for all the girls. "Papa, can we ever meet some fellas?"

He looked at her, and the innocent expression on her face just touched his heart. "You can't be tellin' me that you want to leave me, do ya?"

"Oh no, Papa, I will never leave you, but I would like to meet a fella."

"That makes me happy. I don't want to lose any of my girls for a long, long time. You're all so special to me."

Abby looked at her father. She knew he was just saying that so they wouldn't ask any more questions. It had worked when Abby and Jenny were ten, but the twins were fourteen, and they knew their father too well.

"Why Papa, I thought Mama was your special girl."

"But Papa," Abby said. "Mama was twenty-two when she married you."

"Your mother knew me for a year before we married, and those were different times. And I didn't work on no railroad."

"But you won't let us even meet any men."

"I've told you before: these railroad men are only after one thing."

Abby looked at her father again. "And what would that be, Papa?"

Molly felt the conversation had gone off the main topic, and she had to bring it back.

"Daniel, why don't you let them use the road? After all, they paid you to use it. The proper thing to do would be to let them use the road or return the money."

He didn't answer her but kept eating his breakfast.

Suddenly, a knock came from the front door, and the girls turned their heads.

"I wonder who that can be," Molly said. "Abby, will you see to that?"

"Yes, Mama."

Abby stood up and walked down the hall. When she opened the front door, she found the most handsome man she had ever seen on the other side, smiling at her—tall; dark hair, almost black; bright, blue eyes. Nervous, she froze.

"Good morning," he said. "I was wondering if I could speak with Mr. McVinny?"

Abby wanted to answer, but her mouth wouldn't move. All she could do was smile. To top it off, she felt like a fool. She was sure that he thought something was wrong with her.

"Have I come at a bad time?" he asked. "I can wait outside if it's all right."

Then Molly came into the hall. She smiled and extended her hand to him. "Hello. I'm Mrs. McVinny. Can I help you?"

"Yes ma'am, I hope so. My name is Ryan Lochlan, and I work for the railroad. I came to talk to your husband about giving us permission to use his road to bring supply wagons out to the camp."

"Well, I think we can arrange that. I'll have my husband speak with you. Tell me something, Ryan, have you had your breakfast yet?"

"No, ma'am."

"Well, we'll just have to set you up with a plate. Abby, set a plate near Little Annie for Mr. Lochlan. Mr. Lochlan, this is my daughter Abby."

Again, Abby could only smile like a fool as Ryan politely smiled back.

Molly led Ryan to her husband. "Mr. Lochlan has come to speak with you, Daniel. I think you should at least give him a moment of your time."

Daniel looked at Ryan and sat back in his chair. "All right, young fella. Molly says you want to talk to me, so go ahead. I'll give you a few minutes of my time."

Abby placed a plate of food near Ryan, not meeting his eye. Little Annie tugged at his shirt.

Daniel looked down at her. "Yes?"

"I think you're pretty." She smiled, baring both rows of her teeth.

"Well, I think you're pretty too."

Daniel was losing his patience. "I'm waiting."

"Oh yes, I'm sorry, Mr. McVinny. Well, my name is Ryan Lochlan, and I work for the railroad. We met yesterday."

Daniel nodded and waited for Ryan to continue.

"Yes, I can see you wouldn't forget that. Now, I was told that my bosses gave you four thousand dollars, for use of the road, and then you changed your mind. If you didn't want to honor the deal, why didn't you give back the money?"

"Well, that's an easy one to answer. I didn't give back the money 'cause there wasn't any."

"Excuse me?"

"You can be excused all you want, but there was no money. I was given a sack of money and told not to open it until the railroad was done here and moved on. I put the sack in the stable and let it be for a week or two. Well, you see, I ain't ever seen four thousand dollars. Heck I ain't ever seen five hundred dollars. So I thought I'd go open the sack, take a quick peek, and then close the sack again."

"And the money wasn't there."

"Oh no, there was some money, but only on top of the sack. The rest was cut papers."

Ryan was beginning to see why Lafferty had avoided talking about the two men who'd taken the money to McVinny. But the question was who had the money, Lafferty or the two men?

"I see why you feel you have been cheated, Mr. McVinny. I would like to fix this situation if you'll let me."

Daniel had to admit that Ryan seemed genuinely concerned. "I'm listening, son."

"Well, first I'd like to make an agreement between you and me. You give me the right to use your road once a month to ship supplies to the camp, and I promise you I will replace the money that they took from you."

"And why would I believe you? I know how you railroad people work."

"Because after being thrown off your property, I still came back today with no weapons even though yesterday you aimed your gun at me. I believed that maybe if I sat down and talked this out, we could come to an agreement."

Molly was shocked. "Daniel!"

"Hush, woman, they were going to use the road."

"Daniel, you have no right to use your gun as a weapon against this man. He has come here in peace and has shown nothing but kindness to all of us here. I want to apologize, young man, for my husband's rude behavior. And you can have the use of the road, Mr. Lochlan. After all, I own this property too, and I give my permission."

"Molly, do you know what you're saying?" Daniel asked.

"Yes I do, Daniel, and I have given my agreement to this nice young man. You aimed your gun at him, and now you're treating a guest in our home very rudely."

Daniel was about to protest, but he closed his mouth. He turned his attention back to Ryan. "Well, young fella. Looks like we're in agreement. You can use the road. But don't you be forgettin' you are to lead the wagons through and give me a day's notice. Is it a deal?"

Ryan smiled and offered his hand. "We have a deal. Thank you. Thank you so much."

Back at the camp, Lafferty was in his office when two rather scruffy-looking men by the names of Billings and Stiles came in through the side door. Lafferty looked up from his desk, startled by the shadows of the hulking men.

Lafferty had promised Billings and Stiles twenty percent of the money he'd hired them to steal. Of course, Lafferty had no intention of cutting them in on anything, but he also didn't plan on them returning to his office.

"I thought I told you two to never come here. I don't want anyone thinking we're in on anything. After all, what if the old man identifies you?"

Billings, the older one with a dark beard, slowly walked up to Lafferty, his heavy boots pounding the wooden floor.

"Well, maybe we got tired of waiting for you to come and give us our cut of the money."

"There may be a problem with that now. The new foreman from Boston has been asking a lot of questions. He's smart enough to figure out what happened."

Billings walked over to the window.

"Well, he'll just have to go. I can arrange an accident where he gets killed by a shotgun. We'll pin it on Old McVinny."

"That's a good idea."

"We'll do it now since there's no one here. It will be perfect."

"He's not here. He's at the McVinny farm."

"That's even better. We can get him as he's leaving their farm."

# CHAPTER THREE

The door of the McVinny home opened, and Ryan was the first one out, followed by Molly and the girls.

"Mrs. McVinny, it was a real pleasure to have met you," he said. "Thank you for your kindness in allowing me to meet your beautiful family."

"You're welcome here anytime. It was our pleasure to entertain you. Do come back soon. And please, it's Molly, we don't follow formalities here, and my friends call me Molly."

He smiled at her. "Then Molly it is."

He saw Little Annie looking up at him, and he gathered her in his arms.

"Little Annie, it has been a pleasure meeting you, and I will never forget it. You are the sweetest little girl I know."

Little Annie beamed. "See, Mama, he says I'm sweet."

"I think he is most gallant to say that to you." Molly shook her head at Ryan and laughed. "Don't you go spoiling her, Ryan, or you'll have two girls on your hands."

Molly looked toward Abby then turned back to him with a knowing smile.

"Oh, do you think so?" Ryan asked, smiling back shyly. "I'll remember that."

He mounted his horse and gave them another wave. He took one last look at Abby as he turned to ride down the trail toward the main road.

Molly observed her oldest daughter, who seemed to be still watching as Ryan rode out of sight. She wondered if he could be the stranger she saw in her dreams, who would sweep her daughter off her feet—just as another stranger had done to her twenty-some-odd years before. She had to admit Ryan not only was handsome but also had manners and had noticed Abby.

Daniel came over to her. "I'm sorry I didn't tell you about the money, Molly."

"Why didn't you, Daniel? I knew you would never go back on your word, and this didn't seem like you."

"I thought you'd be upset. After all, you were so happy with the thought of what that money could have gotten."

She put her arm around his waist.

"You silly man. I was thinking of the girls. Daniel, it would've meant they could have so much more than we ever did. More than we can ever give them. We always said we wanted our children to have more than we did."

"Are you sorry for what you don't have?"

"Sorry for what I don't have? Never. I have all I could ever want with you, Daniel. You've given a beautiful home, four beautiful daughters, and a lifetime of love. What more could I ever want?"

When Ryan rode into camp, he went straight to Lafferty's cabin. He knocked on the door and walked in.

Lafferty was sitting at his desk, as usual, and he glanced up from his paperwork with an annoyed expression.

"Well, I see you've made it back," he said as if he was disappointed.

"Yes, and I did find out something interesting. Seems the money that was given to McVinny was not four thousand dollars. Seems that the bag had some money in it but was really stacks of cut paper."

Lafferty glared at him. "Are you trying to say—"

"All I'm trying to say is that money was tampered with before it got to McVinny."

"I see. So there really isn't any one person that we can say took it. It could have happened even up in Boston."

"That's right."

Ryan watched the expression on Lafferty's face, wanting to see if there was any sign that he knew about the money. Lafferty betrayed nothing.

"Well, have you made any progress on the road situation?" he asked.

"Yes, Mr. McVinny has entered an agreement with me that the wagons can use the road, but it's only offered once a month and for supplies."

"An agreement with you? Why you?"

"Well it's simple. He doesn't trust the railroad. After all, he thinks the railroad went back on their agreement with the money. And from what I see, I think that he's right."

"I'll have to see what the brass in Boston says about this."

Ryan crossed his arms. "Do you really want Boston to know about the money?"

Lafferty didn't answer right away. "Why wouldn't I?"

"Whatever you decide, Lafferty. I'm heading to join my crew." He went out the door.

Mick beamed when he saw Ryan. "Ryan! Ryan, you made it back."

Ryan got off his horse, and the men rushed over to welcome him.

"I feel like the conquering hero with this greeting. I only went to see a man about getting to use his road, not to take over his land."

Mick was the first to ask a question. "So tell me, did you get him to agree to let them there wagons to pass?"

"Yes."

The entire crew let out a cheer.

"But, I also said it was only to be used once a month for the supply wagons, meaning that it's not for any other purpose."

"Sure, we understand that, Ryan." Mick looked at the men and winked.

Ryan caught that. "I mean it, Mick. I gave the man my word."

Mick looked disappointed when he realized Ryan was serious.

Three weeks had passed when a wire came to Lafferty from Boston, informing them that the supply wagons were leaving the next day, and that time, they would be carrying the payroll.

Lafferty was about to call for Ryan when he heard a knock on the door and Ryan came in.

"Good, you're here," Lafferty said. "I was going to call for you. The supply wagons are set to leave Boston tomorrow morning, early. I'll expect you to have the road open for them. Mind you, they will be carrying the payroll."

"I'll go out to tell Mr. McVinny. I'll be leading the wagons tomorrow."

"Yes, yes, that's a good idea."

"You forget, Mr. Lafferty. It was part of the agreement that I was to lead the wagons."

Ryan went out the door and headed for his cabin, where his horse was tied.

Mick approached. "Where we going, boss?"

"You're not, I am. I have to go to the McVinny farm. The supply wagons are coming tomorrow. I need to tell the man we will be using his road."

"You sure that's the only reason why you're going back there?"

"What's that supposed to mean?"

"Well, I heard that the old man has some fine-looking daughters."

Ryan raised his eyebrows at Mick. "He does have four daughters. Nice girls, all four."

"Oh, so there are just girls, you say."

"That's all I saw. But if you like, I'll ask them their ages."

Ryan rode off. True, he had to let Daniel know about the supply wagons, but he was looking forward to seeing Miss Abby also. Something about the girl had caught his eye.

He rode up to the house and saw Little Annie on the porch.

She noticed him too and gave him a big wave. "Hi, Mr. Ryan!"

"Hi, princess. Is your daddy home?"

Molly came out to the porch when she heard the voices. She was delighted to find Ryan. "How good to see you."

"I was looking for Daniel, ma'am."

"Little Annie, you go fetch Daddy and tell him Ryan is here to see him. Ryan, do come in. It's been a while since you've been here."

"Hello, Molly. It's good to see you too."

He glanced at the door, hoping to see if Abby would also come out to greet him.

Molly noticed his searching eyes. "She's out back if you'd like to say hello to her."

He smiled at Molly. The woman had read his mind. "Thank you, ma'am."

He went to the back of the house where Abby was feeding the chickens.

With her back turned, she had no idea that Ryan was standing there, watching her.

"Hello, Miss Abby."

She stopped and slowly turned around. There he was, as handsome as ever and smiling at her. Those eyes just seemed to sparkle like thousands of stars. She had not dreamt it—he was the most handsome man she had ever seen.

Feeling dizzy, she walked over, opened the gate, and left the coop. "Mr. Lochlan," she managed to say this time. "This is a nice surprise. What brings you here?"

"I wanted to let your father know that the supply wagons are coming tomorrow, and I'll be here to escort them through his road."

"Oh." She sounded slightly disappointment. "Well, Papa is out tending the sheep. I'd be happy to take you there."

"Little Annie went to get him."

"Oh." Once again, disappointment in her voice.

She blushed. How pretty she was when she blushed.

"But I'm glad she did, 'cause I get to see you," he said quickly. "It's been a while since I've been here, and I kinda missed seeing you. I admit that our first meeting was a bit awkward. I mean me taking you by surprise when you opened the door. I thought at first I had frightened you, but I soon realized it was just surprise. And I thought maybe you'd like to go for a walk tomorrow when I come back. That's if you haven't got anything better to do."

A smile slowly broke out on her face.

Ryan marveled at how lovely her smile was. She had a twinkle in her emerald eyes when she did. He could feel his heart beating more wildly. Could he be falling in love with her already?

How could he not, with a woman that enchanting? He wondered if she might feel something for him too.

From the first moment he saw her, he'd felt he had found his dream, the reason he'd come to America, the meaning to his life. If he was right, all his desires were standing right before him.

Her lashes swept up as she looked up at him again. He felt a magnetic chemistry drawing them together.

"I'd like to take a walk with you," she said sweetly. "Will you be staying for lunch?"

"I don't know, but I will be back tomorrow. You did say yes! And now we have a date."

She only blushed.

Suddenly Daniel's voice came from behind him. "Ryan, how ya be, son?"

"Fine, Daniel, and you?"

"Fine. Molly tells me you be here to tell me about the wagons."

"Well, we had an agreement. I gave you my word."

Daniel looked between Ryan and Abby.

"True, you did give me your word, and I believe you, son. You can use the road for your wagons. When you've taken them through, you bring yerself back and have supper with us."

Ryan's happiness at the offer was irrepressible as he shook Daniel's hand.

"Thank you, sir. Thank you very much."

"Let's go tell Molly. Or is there something else you'd be wantin' to do?"

"No, let's go tell Molly."

# CHAPTER FOUR

From the cliff about a hundred yards away from the McVinny homestead, Lafferty's two hired guns were watching Ryan and Daniel like hawks. They had a good view of the house, even if it was partly blocked by a maple tree.

"Seems something is going on," Billings said.

"Just shoot and get it over with," Stiles said. "We missed him the first time, and we need to finish this job this time 'round."

"No, this is too easy. Besides, I don't trust Lafferty. He hasn't paid us our share for the last job we did. I'm even willing to bet that he's got it in that desk drawer of his in his office."

"Then let's just take it and run."

Billings liked the idea and smiled at his partner.

"Let's get down this cliff. We can be back at the office to get the money and be out of there before he gets back."

Back at the camp, Billings tried to pry open the drawer of Lafferty's desk with his hunting knife. He and Stiles were so busy they didn't notice Lafferty walk in on them.

"I might have guessed you two would come back here and try to steal from me," Lafferty said. "And here I was going to cut you in on this money."

Billings and Stiles stopped in their tracks. Billings had managed to get the drawer open, but there was no money inside. They looked at Lafferty, speechless. Lafferty blinked back at them.

"Yeah, you heard me. Seems the supply wagon is coming tomorrow, and it's carrying the payroll. Now, wouldn't it be a shame if something happened to them wagons."

Billings looked a bit confused at first, then he got it.

"Look, Lafferty, stealing a sack of money was easy, but you're asking us to steal the payroll and the supply wagons. Well, that's something else."

"If you two aren't up to the job, I suppose I can find two others that have a backbone."

Billings's nostrils flared. "We can do this job, but this is the last time. When it's done, we want our share, and we're out of here."

Lafferty gave them his evil smile and laughed.

"Oh, you'll get your cut. Now get out of here and don't let me see you till the job is done."

They started to head out the door when Lafferty stopped them.

"Oh, boys, if you don't get it done, don't bother coming back."

Ryan woke up early and went to the cook's tent for a cup of coffee.

"You're up early, Mr. Ryan," said Cookie, the stout, cheerful chef.

"I have to meet the supply wagons today."

"You be careful. The payroll is on the supply wagons."

Ryan looked at the cook. "Payroll? Who told you that, Cookie?"

"Doggin. He got the telegram and gave it to Lafferty. Every wire that comes in, we know about."

Ryan realized that the news could be all over the camp.

"I see. Well thanks, Cookie. I have to get going."

He'd almost reached the door when Cookie yelled, "What about your coffee?"

"I'll get it next time."

With that, he was off. He went straight back to the cabin, where Mick was sitting on the steps.

"Get your horse and make it fast."

"What's wrong?"

"I said get your horse."

Mick rushed toward the corral. By the time he came back, Ryan was already on his horse. He had a rifle in his hand and tossed it to Mick.

"You're gonna need this," Ryan said. "The payroll is coming on the supply wagon, and I have a bad feeling about this."

"Well, what are we standing around for? Let's get going."

Billings and Stiles took their positions on the ridge again, waiting for Ryan to ride by.

Ryan knew he had to lead the wagons in order to avoid suspicion, but Mick could be the driver on the first wagon. As they waited by the entrance to the road, Ryan ran the plan by Mick.

"Well it's sounds real simple, but how do we know where they're hiding?" Mick asked.

"We'll know when the gunfire takes place."

Mick shook his head. "I like a well-planned operation, and this one is not.'"

"You can always say no."

Mick thought for a minute and relented.

"I still want to meet that old man's daughters. You're going through a lot of trouble for the railroad, and I know you aren't fond of the railroad. I mean, you're like a knight in shining armor, so it has to be a girl. Am I right, Sir Lancelot?"

"What are you talking about?" Ryan played dumb.

"I tell you, she must be some kind of girl."

Ryan couldn't help but smile. "She is, my friend. She truly is."

They heard the wagons in the distance and soon saw them as they turned the bend.

"Okay, Mick, it's time to play hero."

"Hero? Oh no, not me, Sir Lancelot. I'm just here to see her. You're the one who wants to slay the dragon, save the fair maiden, and win her undying love."

The first wagon came to a stop.

"Howdy, Ryan," the driver said. "You giving us an escort across this road?"

"How ya doing, Seth? Yes, but I'm having Mick drive the wagon. I want you in the back, just watching. Too many people know about your cargo this time around."

"Anything you say, Ryan. You expecting trouble?"

"Better safe than sorry," was all Ryan would say.

"I'd rather be in the back," Seth said, "and having Mick up front sure does make me feel better."

Seth went to the back of the wagon, and Mick sat in the front after he tied his horse to a tree limb. Ryan looked around and got ready to lead the wagons.

Mick turned to him. "Okay, let's go be knights of the Round Table."

Slowly, Ryan led the wagons down the barren road.

Billings and Stiles saw them as they turned a bend but waited for a close shot of Ryan.

Suddenly a shot rang out. Ryan jumped from his horse and used the side of the wagon for cover. Mick and Seth jumped down too and ran behind the wagon, beside Ryan.

Mick turned to Ryan. "Where are the shots coming from?"

"I can't be sure, but I think it's from behind that ridge over there."

Seth looked up. "Ryan, if you look to the right, you will see the glare off the barrel of one of the shotguns."

"I don't see it, Seth."

Seth took his hat and put it on the barrel of his rifle. He raised it, and a shot sent it flying toward the nearest branch.

"Do you see it now, Ryan?"

"Yes, now I do, Seth."

"And that was my new hat, too."

"Mick, you go right, and I'll go left. Seth, give us some cover."

"Say when," Mick replied.

"Let's go."

Seth started firing as Ryan and Mick concentrated on the two guns. The sound of bullets rang out in the open air.

# CHAPTER FIVE

Billings had had enough. He knew that if they stayed, they would surely be killed. "Let's get out of here, Stiles."

Billings made his way down the cliff. Stiles was right behind when he took a bullet in the chest that killed him instantly.

Billings looked back with a start. He didn't wait. He took off on his horse.

Ryan shrugged at Mick.

"Guess they've had enough," Mick said.

Ryan called to Seth. "Come on, let's get these wagons moving."

Seth got back on, and soon the wagons were moving down the road again. From nowhere, Daniel came out of the shrubs, and headed their way.

"Ryan my boy, I heard some gunfire. Everthin' all right?"

"Seems someone didn't want us to use your road, Daniel. They were firing at us from that ridge over there."

"If you like, I can give it a look-see."

"No, wait till I get back, Daniel. I'd like to see what I'm up against."

"As you say."

Mick came up behind them after going back to get his horse. "Are we ready, Ryan?"

"Daniel, this is my good friend, Mick Dawson," Ryan said. "He's come along to help me in case of trouble."

Daniel smiled at him. "Glad to meet ya, Mick."

"Same here, Mr. McVinny."

"It's Daniel, son, just plain Daniel. Ryan, bring Mick with you when you come back."

Ryan waved as they both rode away to catch up with the head wagon. They arrived at the camp in no time, much to Lafferty's surprise.

Lafferty wondered what had happened to those two he hired to do the job. He was stuck with the payroll, which could have been all his if they had followed orders. And where were they now? At some pub most likely.

He had to keep up appearances after all, so he walked over to Ryan. "Well, it looks like you made it without a problem."

"Sometimes miracles do happen."

Ryan knew that Lafferty was involved, but he had no proof. Maybe if he had captured one of those gunmen, but one was dead and the other had fled.

Later that day, after they escorted the wagons back, Ryan and Mick stopped at the McVinny farm. Slowly, they made their way down the road, and there on the porch was Little Annie. Her face lit up when she saw them.

"Ryan!"

"That's Little Annie," Ryan told Mick. "She thinks I'm pretty. She likes to give hugs. Her twin sister Mary is a bit more on the quiet side."

The door opened, and Molly came out to the porch.

"That's Mrs. McVinny," Ryan told Mick. "She likes to be called Molly. That's the love of

Daniel's life. As long as Molly likes you, you're safe."

Mick looked back at Ryan. "So where's that special girl that has you dreaming of moonlight and apple blossoms?"

Ryan smiled as she appeared at the door. "There ya go, Mick. That's Miss Abigail McVinny."

The look on Ryan's face told Mick all he needed to know. Abby, her glistening brown hair down to her waist, looked graceful in a pretty lavender dress. Ryan was truly in love with the young girl, and now his friend could see why.

"She is truly beautiful, Ryan. You were right. She could have *me* dreaming of moonlight and apple blossoms."

"Easy there."

They continued to the porch and got off their horses. Molly came down to give Ryan a hug.

"Oh Ryan, it's so good to see you. We heard some gunshots earlier today. Is everything all right?"

"Molly, it really was nothing. The men saw a deer, and they haven't had fresh meat in a while and wanted to take it back to the camp as a surprise for the crew."

Molly looked at him and smiled. She knew he was keeping something from her, but she also knew not to ask. She turned her attention to Mick.

"And who is this fine-looking gentleman? I'm beginning to think the railroad only hires fine-looking men to turn these poor country girls' heads."

"This is my good friend Mick Dawson. I told him about your cooking, and he really could use a good meal, ma'am. Why, he's almost down to skin and bones. He's been eating Cookie's food, and it's pretty bad, ma'am."

"It's true, ma'am. I really could use a real home-cooked meal."

Molly beamed as she took Mick's arm. "Come along, Mick Dawson, and I'll treat you to a home-cooked meal, and mind you, I will know all about you by the time you leave here. And if I like what I find out, I may let you come back again. Did Ryan tell you I have two other daughters?"

"He did mention something about you having four girls."

"I see. He's right. I have four girls." She led Mick into the house.

Abby walked over to Ryan. "The gunshots?" she whispered.

"It was nothing. By the way, where's Jenny?"

"She's in the kitchen. Why?"

"I thought she'd like to meet Mick. I think he would really like to meet her. Maybe all of us can go for a walk. We never really have time to be together, and I thought, with Jenny and Mick, your pa wouldn't object. Do you think you would like that?"

Abby's eyes twinkled as she smiled. "I would love that, some time to be with you. Even with Jenny around."

Abby went off into the kitchen to find her.

Ryan found most of the family in the living room, and he sat on a chair near Little Annie. Mary smiled shyly at Ryan and then turned her attention to her book.

"Ryan," Molly said, "you never told us before you have such a charming friend. You must bring him here more often."

Just then, Abby and Jenny came from the kitchen with refreshments.

"I hope you will join us for some refreshments, Mick. Oh, by the way, this is my second-oldest daughter, Jenny. Jenny, this is Ryan's friend, Mick Dawson."

"Mr. Dawson," Jenny said. She batted her long lashes at him then looked down shyly.

Mick got up to shake her hand. He marveled at Jenny's beautiful blue eyes.

Ryan couldn't help but think of another knight of the Round Table.

When Daniel came back, he was ready for supper. Before he would sit down, he pulled Ryan over to the side.

"Ryan, the feller on the ridge, he was one of the ones who brought me the sack of money."

"Are you sure?"

"Sure I's sure."

"Where is he?"

"I had him placed on the side road on his horse. I figured you'd want to take him back to camp with you."

"Good idea, Daniel."

Ryan looked at Mick and then Molly.

"Molly, I'm sorry, but we really have to get back. I know you just met Mick, but we do have to go back. Since tomorrow is Sunday, I thought we'd spend the whole day with you after service."

"Oh Ryan, that's a wonderful idea, and we'll make it a picnic. Now, promise you won't back out."

"I promise."

She gave him a big hug and kissed his cheek. "You are a sweet soul, Ryan." She gave Mick a hug also. "Mick, you are welcome here also, and I want to see you tomorrow."

"Yes, ma'am."

The boys got on their horses and rode off.

"Why did we leave so early?" Mick asked Ryan.

"Daniel left the body of the gunman from this morning. Daniel says he's one of the men who gave him the sack of money that was filled with paper, not money. Somehow Lafferty was involved in this, only I can't prove it."

They rode into camp with the body of Stiles over his horse. Their first stop was Lafferty's office. Ryan walked up to the door and knocked.

"Come in."

"Lafferty, we have one of the men who shot at the supply wagon this morning. I thought you would like to see him."

"Ah, yes. Bring him in."

"Sorry, sir, he's dead."

"Oh. Well, in that case, I'll be right out."

Lafferty walked around the horse and lifted the blanket covering the body to see the man's face.

"Yes, that's one of the men that I gave the money to take to McVinny." Lafferty's expression was neutral.

Ryan looked at him closely. "Thanks, Lafferty. Maybe when we find the other gunman, we can find the missing money."

"Yes. That would make sense."

# CHAPTER SIX

On a bright, sunny morning, Mick and Ryan headed to the McVinny farm.

"Do you think Jenny could like me?" Mick asked.

"What's not to like? After all, you're a hero. That is, after me, of course."

"Of course."

"So, is sweet little Jenny making Sir Galahad think—how did you say it—moonlight and roses?"

"Apple blossoms. I just asked if she'd like me, nothing more."

Ryan gave Mick a knowing look, and they continued.

At the house, the girls were getting in the wagon for church. Mary and Little Annie sat in the back while Jenny and Abby were in the seat before Molly and Daniel.

The girls were chatting excitedly, talking about how they couldn't wait to see Ryan and Mick. Molly beamed at them while listening. She was happy for her daughters. The girls were getting older, and Molly felt they should be meeting men. Molly had told Daniel he couldn't keep them with him forever.

They turned the bend, and Molly looked over at her husband with a smile, the same smile that he had fallen in love with twenty-some years before. They all were waiting to see Ryan and Mick around the next corner. The sun was shining on her face, giving it an angelic glow.

Suddenly, shots rang out. Molly's body jerked forward, a look of shock frozen in her eyes. Her body slumped back as strands of her auburn hair flew over her face.

Abby reached for her mother but heard Mary scream and turned toward her. Jenny noticed Little Annie slumped to the side. Her face was ashen, and the life went out of her soft eyes, leaving them a blank stare. Annie was gone as soon as a bullet hit her.

Daniel cried out, beside himself with his dear Molly slumped across the seat and his sweet Annie dead.

Ryan and Mick heard the shots and raced to the source. They got there to find Daniel cradling Molly's lifeless body. Ryan looked past him and saw Abby holding the body of Little Annie. He had to turn his head to hide his tears. He had just been talking to her not too long ago, and now his Little Annie was dead. Mick too was overcome when he saw the bodies of Molly and Annie.

Daniel looked at Ryan with emptiness in his eyes. "She's gone, Ryan. Someone took my Molly away. Find who did this, Ryan. Find them and make them pay."

"I promise you," Ryan said. "I will find them, and we will both make them pay."

"Ryan, we have to take them back home," Abby pleaded. "Please don't let them stay here like this."

He turned back to Daniel. "Take Molly in your arms, and I'll turn the wagon around and bring you all back home."

Daniel hung his head and moved over.

Ryan stepped onto the wagon. He turned it around to bring it back to the house, where he brought the wagon to a halt. He jumped out to help Daniel with Molly. Slowly, Daniel handed Molly's body to Ryan. He carried her gently and with great tenderness into the house.

Ahead of him, Jenny opened the door and led him into her parents' bedroom. As he placed Molly's body on the bed, he saw that the bullet had passed through her body and realized it had probably then hit Annie.

Mick was holding Annie as Abby led him to the other bedroom. As Mick came out, leaving Abby in the room, he stopped by to have a word with Ryan.

"I want to know who did this. I want to know why, and I want them," Mick growled.

Mary walked into the house, dry eyed. She had just seen her mother and sister killed in front of her, and everything seemed beyond control. She sat silently by the door. Daniel sat at the table, looking toward the bedroom where Molly was lying.

Ryan had to find out who did this, but he had another problem.

"We can't leave them like this," Ryan said to Mick, "but we just can't stay and let whoever did this run free."

"Ryan, why would someone do this? I mean, Molly and Annie, they never hurt anyone. They were kind and loving people. Molly, my God... She was a saint, and Annie, she..."

He stopped and walked over to the window to regain his composure.

Mary came over to them when she saw them talking. She gently tugged at Ryan's shirt.

"It was the man who was at the end of the road last week."

"A man was here last week, sweetie?"

She nodded. "He had very little hair and holes in his face."

Ryan and Mick looked at each other, and both said, "Lafferty."

"Ryan, you stay here," Mick said. "I'll handle Lafferty."

"Mick, you don't know—"

"Well, if I stay here, we'll never know, and he'll be gone."

Lafferty, back at camp, was clearing out everything he had. He had to get away and leave nothing behind that would lead any of these crimes to him. Billings and Stiles had made too many mistakes, and with Stiles dead, it wouldn't be too long before old McVinny pointed him out as one of the men who'd brought him the sack of paper money. If Billings was caught, he would save his own hide and point the finger at Lafferty. He had to get out and get out fast while everyone was still away from the camp.

He quickly jumped on his horse and started to ride off, making sure he used roads that were well traveled, to mask the tracks.

He'd been riding for some time when he decided he'd gone far enough and needed to rest for the night. He soon came to a place known as the Bridgewater Triangle.

Some had said that the area was haunted. Many stayed away from the swamp, and others told stories of what went on there. But Lafferty didn't believe in ghosts or anything of that sort. He'd heard that the Wampanoag tribe had placed a curse on the swamp for all the suffering the white man had put them through. Many said that they'd witnessed paranormal disturbances, from flashing lights to creatures to strange voices coming from the swamp.

Around midnight, Lafferty was awakened by the sound of voices. He looked around but saw no one. Thinking what he'd heard was just a dream, he decided to go back to sleep. He felt a chill, and the hairs on his neck stood up, which prompted him to put another log on his fire, to take the chill out of the air, but that didn't help.

Then the voices came again. They seemed to be getting closer and were followed by gunfire. He was more startled this time, fearing he was going to be arrested for robbing the railroad money.

He jumped up and began to run. His heart was beating rapidly, and he was having trouble breathing. He ran over to his horse, but something spooked it.

A flash of light appeared, and the light seemed to glide away from him as if it had a life of its own. Lafferty tried to run after it, but in the dark, he ran into the swamp.

Deeper and deeper he went until he felt stuck.

He started to sink. He cried out for help, but no one was around to hear him. He knew this was the end for him.

Alone in the dark, Miles Lafferty died in the quicksand. All there was left of his existence was a sack of money, the same sack of money that was to go to Daniel.

Was it the curse of the Wampanoag Tribe, a guilty mind, or justice that drove Lafferty into the swamp? Nobody would ever know.

Mick did go back to camp, but Lafferty wasn't there. No one had seen him since the morning. Mick had sent out a number of wires to other railroads and then a wire to his bosses in Boston.

With Lafferty gone, they needed a new head foreman, and Mick suggested Ryan for the job. Of course, the decision would have to be put to the board and voted on, but with Mick's strong recommendation, Ryan was sure to get the job—if he wanted it, of course.

# CHAPTER SEVEN

All was silent in the McVinny home. Hardly anyone spoke, whether they were still or moving about.

Daniel was sitting beside Ryan at the table. "Who could have done this, Ryan? Why would they want to hurt my Molly and Annie?"

"I don't know, Daniel. I really don't know."

As Ryan looked around the room, it seemed very empty. Without Molly's laughter and charm, it really was just four plain wooden walls. Her grace and love had turned that house into a home that welcomed all who walked through the front door. With her gone, that magic was also gone.

Each time Ryan thought of Little Annie, tears filled his eyes. With her happy smile and soft brown eyes, she'd been a princess. She'd always brought a smile to his face. Her smile would be only a memory, a memory he would carry in his heart until they met again.

Abby walked into the room, looking as though she hadn't slept for days. She was the rock everyone went to, but she didn't look all there.

Ryan stood up and rushed over to her. "You look like you could use some fresh air."

She didn't disagree, and he opened the door to the porch. She walked outside and stopped by a chair. Slowly, she moved her hand over the arms of the chair, remembering her mother sitting on it.

Ryan wished he could say or do something to ease the pain, but he too was feeling that same pain.

She looked up at him. "She loved sitting here and looking at her flower garden. She loved her roses. They were her favorite."

With those last words, her voice cracked, and tears filled her eyes. Ryan gently drew her close.

"I miss her so, Ryan. I just don't know what..."

"It's hard, I know, but we'll all get through it."

They heard the sound of a wagon heading up the dirt road. Mick was the driver. As he drew closer and pulled the horses to a stop, Ryan noticed something in the back. Mick jumped off and lifted the tarp from the wagon to reveal two coffins.

"Miss Abby," he said, "I took the liberty of getting these for your dear mother and young sister."

"Oh, thank you so much, Mick."

"I wanted to do something for your family."

Ryan went over to look at the coffins. Mick had gotten their names burnt into the wood. "That is thoughtful, Mick."

They each grabbed an end and slowly eased the coffins out, one at a time. With Abby leading the way, they took them into the proper rooms.

Later on that day, Molly and Annie were laid to rest not far from the home. Jenny read from the Bible, and Mary placed roses on the graves while Abby stood by her father's side.

"Abby's a strong girl, Ryan," Mick whispered, "but the deaths are starting to take a toll on her."

"I know, Mick."

As Mick passed by the dining table, he saw Daniel sitting there with his head down. He walked over to the old man.

"Daniel, how are you doing?"

"Hello, Mick. I didn't see you come in."

He tried to get up but fell back down as soon as he did. Stress over the recent tragedies had made his body weak.

"Daniel, let's just sit here for a while," Mick said. "I'll have Jenny get you something to drink."

"You know, Molly always wanted to be the first to greet the guests when they came to the house."

Ryan came over and sat across from them.

Daniel turned to Ryan. "I was just telling Mick how Molly always was one to greet people, how she did love to greet people." He looked at both men and smiled sadly. "We was just sayin' a few days ago how it's time the gals start gittin' out more." His eyes glazed over at the memory. "My Molly reminded me of that social we met at. I know yous boy have heard it before, but boys, I tells ya, she was by far the prettiest gal I ever did see. She had this smile, and let me tell..."

He paused for a moment, remembering the woman he loved. He turned to Ryan. "It's the way you and Abby look at each other. Molly was the first to notice it. But then again, you know how women are and how they kin tell things. Abby was as wild as a young filly, and one look at you, and well, you see."

He smiled for the first time since the accident. Ryan was relieved, for he had been worrying about the old man.

A knock came from the door. Jenny answered it and then entered the dining room to hand an envelope to Mick.

"A gentleman said to give this to you, Mr. Dawson," she said.

"Thank you."

Ryan turned to him with a questioning look.

"It's a long story, Ryan. I'll tell you later." Mick opened the envelope and read the contents. "They found Lafferty's horse and belongings by the swamp near the Bridgewater Triangle. No sign of Lafferty though, but with his belongings was a sack full of money—exactly four thousand dollars' worth. Looks like we found your money, Daniel."

"Why do I get the feeling you're just not some worker?" Ryan said, narrowing his eyes at his buddy.

"Well, to tell you the truth, Ryan, I'm not. I'm a private security officer for the railroad."

"And you didn't want to let me in on this?"

"I wanted to, Ryan, but I just couldn't! The less who knew, the safer the plan would be."

"The plan... Was this all part of a *game*?"

Their voices had been getting louder. Jenny and Abby came out of the kitchen, and Jenny came over to stop their arguing.

"Will you two remember where you are? This is not the time or place to fight. I suggest you go outside until you've cooled off."

They obeyed, shutting the door behind them.

"Alright, Mick, what couldn't you tell me before now?"

"Well, you now know I work for the railroad as a private agent."

"And you were going to tell me this when?"

"I couldn't tell anyone. I had my orders."

Ryan just couldn't understand how that man, who'd been by his side all those months, was his friend but had been lying about his identity the whole time.

"Tell me, Mick, were Molly and Annie part of the plan also? Did they have to die to prove a point?"

"Ryan, don't be crazy. Do you think I would ever put Molly and Annie's lives in danger?"

"I don't know, Mick. You tell me."

Abby came outside with a lethal expression. In a deadly voice hardly above a whisper, she demanded, "What are you two doing? My mother and baby sister are not even cold in the grave. Have you no compassion for what we are going through?"

"Abby, he's a private agent for the railroad!"

"I don't care if he's the king of England! Both of you keep your voices down. If you won't do it for us, do it for my mama and Annie."

With that, she charged back into the house.

Mick looked at Ryan. "She's right, you know. This isn't the time or place."

Mary came out next. "Why are you two making Abby cry? I thought you loved her, Ryan? Mama said you did, and here you go and make her cry. Why?"

Ryan sighed. "I'm sorry."

"Go ahead, Ryan," Mick said. "I'll explain this to the others."

Ryan went into the house to look for Abby. She wasn't inside.

In the backyard, he found her feeding a lamb whose mama had passed giving birth to her. Abby had taken on the job of feeding her until she was old enough to fend for herself.

Ryan slowly walked up to her. "Abby?"

She raised her eyes toward him. "I really don't want to talk to you right now, Ryan."

"I'm sorry. I was wrong, Abby, I just didn't..."

She placed the lamb back inside its pen. "You didn't think my mama loved you? And good Lord, Annie... She thought you were some knight in shining armor. For both of you to argue..." She stopped and turned around to hide her tears.

"I was wrong. I'm sorry. I just was taken by surprise at—"

"Sometimes you are so long-winded. Must be a trait of the Irish, or did you kiss the Blarney Stone?"

"And how would you know about the Blarney Stone?"

"Have you forgotten my last name is McVinny, Mr. Lochlan?"

A hint of a smile appeared on her face, and Ryan knew she had cooled off.

"So tell me, sweet Abby, have you forgiven me?"

"I'm not sure."

He pulled her in and took her in his arms. She looked into his eyes.

"When will you know for sure?" he asked softly.

He slowly lowered his lips to hers and gently kissed her.

Oh, that first kiss, the one every girl dreamt of and looked forward to...

For Abby, it was just that.

As Ryan drew back, she had her eyes closed as she savored the sensation, which could never be replaced. She knew that he was the man she would spend the rest of her life with. No other man would ever make her feel that way.

She looked into his bright blue eyes and knew he felt the same way.

"I have wanted to do that since the first day I saw you," Ryan murmured. "I think it's your eyes. They seem to draw me into your world."

"Really? You never showed any interest."

He looked at her with surprise. "I didn't have anything to offer you, and I didn't want your family to think I was only after you because you had all this."

"Oh that's not true. You know my mama loved you. I think she had you picked out the first day you came here. She was impressed by how you stood up to Papa. Not many men stand up to Papa, and not too many ever come here."

He took her hand, and they walked back to the house.

When they went in the back door smiling, everyone saw they were no longer mad.

"Everything okay with you two?" Mick asked.

Before Ryan could answer, shots rang out again.

Jenny fell on top of Mary to protect her, Mick pulled Daniel to the floor, and Ryan shielded Abby with his body.

Ryan looked over at Mick. "Well, we know this is not Lafferty."

"Abby, are there any guns in the house?"

"Papa has two in the bedroom closet."

"Mick, stick with them. I'll be right back."

Ryan crawled down the hall and made his way to the bedroom closet. Strangely, they heard no more shots, but the shooter might still have been out there.

"We have to draw him away from the house and keep Daniel and the girls safe," Ryan said to Mick.

"All right, which way—front door or back?"

"Front," he told Abby, "Close this door when we leave and don't open it for anyone. Do you understand?"

"But what if—"

"Do you understand what I just said? Do not open it for anyone."

She nodded. "Yes."

He made his way to the door, turned back to Abby, and took her beautiful face in his hands. "Just in case you forget, I love you. Just hold on to that until I get back."

He kissed her and headed out the door, followed by Mick.

Inside the house, they heard shots and then silence.

Abby waited and prayed that she would hear Ryan's voice, yet minutes passed without a sound. Her heart began to pound, and she felt an uncontrollable urge to open the door and call out his name. Still, she'd promised him she wouldn't. She thought of her mother and asked her to watch over Ryan. The shots seemed to stop, and the silence was almost too much to bear.

Suddenly, she heard footsteps on the porch. She held her breath, and then Ryan's voice called out.

"Abby, open the door. Mick's been hit."

She quickly unlatched the lock, and Ryan helped Mick inside.

Mick had taken a bullet in the leg, but it was a clean wound that went right through. Jenny rushed over as they helped him to the sofa.

"Hey Ryan, didn't you tell her not to open the door for anyone?" Mick joked weakly.

"I did, didn't I?"

"Well, you called me by my name, so I opened it," she said. "You did say Mick was hit also."

Mick started to laugh. "I can see it's gonna be an interesting life with you two."

Abby looked at Ryan. "Did you find out who was shooting at us?"

"It was the same one who shot at us two days ago when he killed your mother and Annie. Seemed he had no idea that Lafferty was dead, and he was hired by him to kill me. He confessed everything before he died. He also said Lafferty had planned the whole thing, from stealing the money from the sacks that were to go to Daniel to planning to steal the payroll wagon for a big score." Ryan's face was dark. "I'm so sorry, Abby. It was all my fault. Can you ever forgive me?"

Abby's eyes were still full of tears. Her mother and sister were dead, but she couldn't blame Ryan. He was the love of her life, and he wasn't the one who pulled the trigger.

"Of course. Of course I forgive you. It's not your fault."

Ryan embraced Abby and smelled the sweet perfume of her hair.

Their romance officially began that day. Everyone had been waiting for the two of them to admit it to themselves. Lord knew they had eyes only for each other.

Even Daniel liked the boy. He felt Ryan was a good match for Abby, and he had not met many men suitable for his daughter.

Ryan and Mick became frequent guests for Sunday supper.

# CHAPTER EIGHT

During the next six months, Abby and Ryan spent most of their time together. Since Ryan had retired from the railroad, he had more time to help Daniel on the farm and see Abby. With his previous experience working on his father's farm, Ryan found the work enjoyable. It also kept him close to Abby every day.

Mick had been sent back to Boston but still found time to be down on weekends to see Jenny.

Daniel liked the fact that both girls had found fine men. Even Mary was going to socials after Abby and Jenny had persuaded Daniel to let her go.

Abby chose the last day of summer to be the day of her wedding. The heat and humidity had subsided during this time, and one was still able to have an outdoor ceremony.

The invitations were sent, the announcements were made, and that was the day Abby would become Mrs. Ryan Lochlan.

In private, she would say her new name over and over again until it just rolled off her tongue. She loved the sound of it.

The guests started to arrive at the house early in the morning. The railroad crew had built a platform for the service to take place on. Jenny and Mary had done a wonderful job decorating.

Nora and Paul Kelly had arrived and were greeted on the porch by Abby and Ryan. Nora had made the wedding cake for the couple, and what a beautiful cake it was, with vanilla frosting and blue roses. As their wagon stopped in front of the house, Ryan stepped off the porch and helped Nora off the wagon.

"Nora, you're lovelier than I remember," he said. "'Tis a shame that I'm getting married today."

"Now Ryan, you know that's not true." She gave him a hug. "Child, I swear you are too handsome for your own good. I know a lot of hearts are broken today with you getting married."

"I want you to meet Abby."

He led her upstairs, where Abby greeted them with her beautiful smile.

"Abby, this is my dear Nora Kelly," he said, "the only woman I would ever leave you for if she is available."

Nora smiled, a bit embarrassed. "Don't listen to him, Abby. I'm happy to meet you. I wanted to come here today to meet the lucky girl who caught this fine prince. I knew you were something special, and now that I see you, I can see why."

"Thank you." Abby blushed.

Nora and Abby walked into the house, followed by Ryan and Paul carrying the cake.

After the cake was in place, Ryan introduced Paul to Daniel. The men started talking and soon became close friends.

The musicians arrived. They started playing outside, and music began to fill the house. Father Cahill was talking with Papa and Ryan while everyone was waiting for the bride. The father had baptized all three girls, and watched them grow up. This wedding was a special day for him as well. He was happy for Abby.

As was expected, Mick was best man, and Jenny was maid of honor. Mary was happy not being in the wedding party because she got to enjoy it, although she helped by greeting the guests and helping them find their seats.

Abby went up the stairs to prepare for her wedding. Her wedding. Yes, even when she said the word it sounded like a dream—a dream that a year ago had seemed far away. Now in just a few hours, she would step outside for the ceremony, and her life would be transformed forever. She was going to share her life with a man she loved with her whole heart and soul.

Molly had always loved special events, and the wedding day of her oldest daughter... Oh, how Molly would have beamed with pride if she could've seen her.

A gentle breeze entered Abby's bedroom and brushed Abby's cheek. She heard her name pronounced softly, then it was gone along with the breeze. She looked around. No one was in sight, but she knew there had been. She'd felt it.

"Thanks, Mama, for being here today," she whispered.

She often felt her mother's presence. She couldn't explain it to anyone except her sisters. Mary also felt that Annie was with her sometimes.

"I know you're happy, Mama. It's one of those special days you and Papa always talked about—the days you would see your girls begin a life, a new chapter in their lives and know the love both of you shared. He misses you so, and so do we, Mama."

A light tap came from the door, and Daniel walked in. Abby hadn't seen her father look that handsome for as long as she could remember. His hair had been cut and brushed neatly, and his usual stubble shaved clean. Seeing him standing there, she understood what her mama had seen when she first met him and why she had fallen in love with him.

"Oh my, Abby. You look just like your dear mother."

"Do you think so, Papa?"

Tears filled his eyes as he remembered the day he'd seen his Molly in a wedding dress. "I wish she was here to see you."

She walked over and gave him a hug. "She is, Papa. She is."

"I feel her too. Always have. She's always with me, just like she promised."

He patted her hand and smiled. "We'd better git down there. Can't keep 'em waitin'."

"Don't worry, Papa, they can't start without me."

She put her arm through his and walked out the door, mere steps away from being Mrs. Lochlan.

As they left the room, a misty fog moved from the mirror to the window, and a woman's whisper was heard. "My sweet Abby, you are so right. I'm always with you and your sisters."

The mist left through the open window and went down to the backyard.

Abby and her father arrived on the back porch.

"Okay, Papa, let's show these people how pretty we look."

"I'm ready."

Ryan was standing at the end of the platform. He couldn't contain the smile on his face when he saw her. She couldn't break her gaze at him either.

Even among the crowd, Ryan and Abby only saw each other. Abby understood how her mother felt when she had fallen in love with her Daniel at first sight.

In the moment Abby had seen Ryan that first day, the moment she opened that front door and he asked to speak to her father, she had fallen in love with that handsome stranger. She had wished he would feel the same, and he did.

As they became man and wife, the sunlight came through the trees and surrounded them with a warm glow of amber light.

Abby looked up, smiled, and whispered, "Thanks, Mama."

The reception came immediately after the ceremony. Ryan was surprised to see one of the big brasses from Boston at the reception. Mr. and Mrs. Herbert Ely made their way through the reception line to greet the couple.

Mr. Ely offered his hand to Ryan. "So happy to be here, Lochlan. The wife and I were planning a cruise into New York, and we decided to squeeze in your little event while waiting for the ship to arrive."

"Thank you for coming, Mr. Ely. May I present my wife, Abigail."

Abby had heard his remark to Ryan, and she wasn't going to let that slide by. She extended her hand and put on her best smile.

"Thank you so much, Mr. Ely, for taking the time from your busy schedule to fit us in while waiting for your ship. I do hope you have time to enjoy some cake at least, but if not, maybe we can send some back to Boston with the Kellys and leave it at your home."

Mr. Ely was speechless at Abby's suggestion. Mrs. Ely huffed.

Abby was the only one pleased. *That will teach you to make my day look unimportant,* she thought.

The time came for the couple's first dance, and as the band played a waltz, Abby turned to Ryan.

"You do know how to dance, don't you?"

"Not a step."

"How can you stand there and tell me that, as an Irishman, you can't dance?"

"Never learned."

She shook her head. "Folks, it seems my husband never learned how to dance, so I'm asking my papa to show him how easy it is. Papa, will you dance with me?"

Daniel stood up. "Not to worry, gal, I'll teach the boy how to dance."

The music started again, and Daniel and his daughter waltzed across the dance floor. Ryan watched and saw how easy it really was. Daniel smiled at him to encourage him to come out and dance with his wife.

Daniel gave his daughter's hand to Ryan. The groom started dancing with his new bride. He stared in her eyes the entire time, feeling as if he had been dancing all his life.

"Are you happy, Mrs. Lochlan?" he asked.

"I could never be happier than I am right now. You've given me a dream I never want to awaken from."

"Oh, but it's not a dream, Abby love. It's real and forever."

He twirled her around the dance floor, and everyone could see that they were in their own world.

# CHAPTER NINE

Time passed, six months to be exact. The young couple was over the moon when they found out Abby was expecting her first child.

Another big excitement was Jenny's engagement. Mick had become part of the family the day he came with Ryan.

Jenny would go anywhere Mick went, but she hoped he would stay in Fall River. She wanted to be there when Abby's baby was born.

Mary was getting older, and she wanted to see the world, to touch the stars and more. Jenny had taken her to New York for her sixteenth birthday. Like a child in a candy store, Mary couldn't believe all the sights and sounds of such a big city. New York was all she talked about for weeks afterward, and she couldn't wait to go back again.

Daniel had been slowing down. With Ryan as top hand, a lot of the work was his to do. True, Daniel still had the last word, but he was getting tired, and he still missed Molly. He had always thought they would grow old together and watch the roses and enjoy their grandchildren. Without his beloved wife, the roses didn't seem so important, and his future grandchildren would never get to know their grandmother.

Abby would see her father depressed every day and wonder if she could do anything to help him. She had hoped the baby would cheer him up, but he just sat in his rocking chair day after day.

The winter set in with a bitter wind. The snowstorms were more like blizzards. They were relieved just to make it out to the barn safely. Ryan had to tie a rope to the back porch and then to himself to get to the barn and back. They heard Jed Jefferson strayed too far from his rope, and it snapped off, and it took him so much time to find his way back he nearly froze to death.

It was a cold and bitter night with the wind halloing when a lone wagon made its way up the road to the McVinny house. Ryan looked out the window and saw a man and a woman get out of the wagon. He opened the door and helped them in.

Despite the winter chill, the man's complexion was sallow. His nose was turned up, almost like a pig's, and he had dark beady pig eyes too. The woman was tall, towering over her male companion, and she had a long, horse-like face.

The man removed his hat and scarf. "Thank you so much. We've been on the road for hours. We're looking for the McVinny farm."

Ryan took his coat and then the woman's. "Well, you're in luck. This is the McVinny farm."

The young man looked at the walls and at the woman.

"'Tis a grand place. It truly is."

Abby spoke up. "May I ask—why are you looking for the McVinny farm?"

"Oh, I'm terribly sorry. My name is Travis McVinny. My uncle's Daniel. Oh, he might not even know I was born. I'm his brother Sean's son."

Abby was surprised and didn't know how to deal with the new information.

"Ryan, go get Papa. Mr. McVinny, would you care to come into the living room and warm yourself by the fire?"

"That would be lovely, darlin'. And who would you be?"

"Abigail. Abigail McVinny Lochlan."

"Ah, a distant cousin, I take it."

Just then, Ryan came back in with Daniel.

"What's all this about, Abby? Ryan says there's someone here saying they's be a McVinny."

"And that be true," said the visitor. "I am Travis McVinny, youngest son of Sean, and me wife Elizabeth. And who be ye?"

"I be Daniel McVinny, and I don't know any Travis or Sean."

"Ye can't be telling me that you're not the son of Travis and Colleen McVinny."

"I'm tellin' ya I'm the son of Michael and Mary Anne McVinny. So if you think I'm any kin of yours, you's be wrong."

Travis looked at Daniel then at his wife. "Well, it looks as we've made a trip for nothing, Elizabeth. I'm sorry to have bothered ye."

"We'll be on our way," she said.

Abby turned to her father. "Papa, you can't send these people out in this cold. Even if they are not kin, at least let them rest until the storm blows over. You know Mama would let them stay."

Daniel realized she was right.

"I'm sorry, son. My wife would never turn someone away. So you and the missus are welcome to spend the night here until the storm stops."

Travis smiled at Daniel. "Thank you very much."

Elizabeth noticed Abby's belly. "When is the little one due?"

"Oh, I've got another four months yet. Tell me, why are you in this snowstorm?"

"It was Travis's idea to come and see your father. He was so insistent that your father was his kin."

"I'm sorry that you came all this way and were wrong," Abby said. "My papa's family were in Virginia. Then, when Papa married, he came here."

"I'm sorry too. 'Tis a lovely place."

"Would your husband be needin' a job? Maybe we could help you find something here."

"He doesn't seem to know much about farming, but he does know bookkeeping."

"Well, maybe we can find something in that. Something will come up. It always does."

"We'll see. Thank you for your help."

Morning came. The snowdrifts had totally covered the porch. As Ryan opened the front door, a good three feet of snow came into the hallway. Abby came into the hall and saw the snow.

"Ryan, is there a reason why there's all this snow in the hall?"

"I opened the door, and it came in."

"Why did you open the door?"

"To see how much snow we had."

When Mary walked past the spare room used by the McVinnys who'd come in the night before, she overheard them talking.

"How long do you think you can play this role of kin to this backwoods bumpkin?" the woman asked.

"Listen, Liz, somewhere in this house, that old man has hidden four thousand dollars, and I plan on finding it and taking it."

"Just because your stupid father told you he has it doesn't make it so. After all, if he knows it's here, why didn't he get it?"

"It's hard to get something when you have shots being fired at you."

Mary quietly stepped away to go down the stairs. She ran into Ryan, who was having a cup of coffee.

"Ryan, I need to talk to you."

"What's wrong, Mary?"

"Those two people upstairs—they're after Papa's four thousand dollars."

Ryan blinked at her. "I knew there was something wrong. I have to tell Abby."

Just then Abby walked in the room. "Tell Abby what?"

Mary blurted it out. "They're lying. They want Papa's money. They know about the four thousand."

Abby took her dad's shotgun from a corner and headed for the stairs.

"Abby, what are you doing?" Ryan whispered loudly.

"Getting those people out of my house!"

Ryan tried to grab the gun from her, but she was holding on to it tightly. "Have you lost your mind? If you won't think of yourself, think of the baby. Give me the gun, Abby."

"Ryan, these people come here to rob us, and you tell me I can't throw them out?"

He shook his head. "I see I'm gonna have a lot of trouble with you. First, you don't have to do this. You have a husband to take care of this kind of stuff. Second, you are carrying my child, which I would like to see be born, but if you try to shoot people, that might not happen."

She released the shotgun, sat down, and put her head in her hands. Just then, Jenny came down and saw something was going on. Travis and Elizabeth came into the kitchen too and noticed the same.

"Good mornin' to ya," Travis said innocently.

Abby looked at him. "You can stop the accent, Travis, or whatever your name is. We know why you're here. Sorry to disappoint you, but there is no money. Our pa was cheated out of it by two men named Lafferty and Billings. When Lafferty died, the money went back to the railroad since the bag had the railroad's name on it."

"That's a lie. My father said it was here. Your pa had it hidden."

"Your pa's a liar. He was the one who gave my papa a bag full of cut paper and gave Lafferty the money."

Travis scowled at her. "I still say you're a liar."

Elizabeth turned to Abby with her sour, horsey face and spat, "Look, there must be something of value in this rat hole. I don't plan on leaving here empty handed."

"Well, I hate to disappoint you, but there is nothing!"

As they were talking, they didn't see Daniel coming in the back door with a pail in his hand. He had just come from milking the cow. He immediately heard what was going on and threw the pail of milk on them, taking them by surprise.

Elizabeth screamed.

Both he and Ryan proceeded to throw the two of them out of the house.

"Now, I suggest you take this wagon and get as far away from here as you can," Ryan said.

"How can we go anywhere with the snow?" Elizabeth sniffled.

Daniel grabbed his shotgun and pointed it at them.

"I think you best listen to me, son in law, 'cause I get a bit testy with folks who come to me and are liars."

# CHAPTER TEN

The first signs of spring appeared. The air was warmer, and the snowdrops and crocuses were popping out of the ground. Daniel was in the barn, milking the cow, when he heard Abby yelling for help. Jenny went running up the stairs, and Daniel followed.

"Papa, the baby's coming," Abby said.

"All right Abby, stay calm. Jenny, go get me plenty of towels and hot water. Mary, go find Ryan. He's somewhere in the north field."

Abby looked at her father. "You do know what you're doing, Papa?"

"Heck, girl, who do you think helped with birthin' you and your sisters?"

"Right, I forgot."

She closed her eyes with the next contraction. Jenny kept taking towels upstairs as Ryan came running in.

"Is she okay?" he asked Jenny.

Suddenly, Abby screamed, and Ryan ran up the stairs and into the room.

As soon as Daniel saw him, he started firing orders. "If you want to be of some use here, hold her hand and let her squeeze it when the pain gets too bad."

"Isn't there something you can do to stop the pain?"

"Ryan, if you want to help, do as I say or git downstairs and let Jenny come here."

Ryan left the room and went to get Jenny. The hours pressed on—twelve hours in labor and still no baby. Ryan was getting worried. A knock came from the front door, and Mary answered it to find Mick.

"Hi, pretty one," Mick told her.

"Hi, Mick. Ryan's in the kitchen, and Abby's having her baby."

With that information, Mick headed straight to the kitchen. "I hear Abby's in labor. Who's with her?"

"Daniel."

They heard the distinct cry of a baby.

"There you go, Lancelot. A new fair maiden."

Jenny came running down for more water when Ryan stopped her.

"Well, Jenny?"

"It's a girl so far."

She ran back up the stairs, and Mary followed.

"What did she mean so *far*?" Ryan asked.

Mick handed him a cup of coffee. "We'll soon find out."

At the sound of another cry, Mary came out. "Ryan, you have twin girls," she exclaimed.

Mick hugged Ryan. Before they could get too excited, they heard another cry, and that time, Daniel came out.

"Ryan, you have three girls and just about the prettiest next to my three I ever did see. Well, come on up here and see them. You too, Mick."

They raced up the stairs as Daniel and Mary headed down to get themselves cups of coffee.

Inside the room, Jenny was holding one of the girls, and Abby had the other two in her arms. Mick walked over to the bed and gave

Abby a kiss on the forehead. He peered down at the two girls in her arms.

"Abby, they are beautiful. I'm so glad because I hoped that they didn't look like Ryan."

Mick went over to pay attention to the baby Jenny was holding.

Ryan slowly came over to his wife with a dumbfounded expression on his face.

"Abby, you always amaze me. Three girls. I suppose you have the names picked out, too."

"Well, these two are Molly and Annie, and the pretty little one over there is Meghan."

Meghan was Ryan's mother's name.

"How did you..." He looked at Mick. "You told her."

Mick shrugged. "Well, she asked, and after all, it's a pretty name for a pretty girl."

Daniel came back up the stairs with Mary, to join everyone.

Abby said, "Papa, we have decided on the names. This is Little Molly." She handed Molly to him. "This one is Annie." She handed Annie to Mary.

Jenny went over to Ryan and handed him the last one.

"And that one is Meghan."

Ryan looked at his daughter cuddled comfortably in his arms, and tears rolled down his cheeks. "I wish my mom was here to see this. She's so beautiful." He turned back to his wife. "Thank you so much, Abby, for giving me my girls."

From that day on, the house was never the same. Six females under one roof was more than any man could take. Though Ryan and Daniel loved their girls, there came a time every man needed some quiet. Their favorite place was a fishing hole that Daniel had come upon years before when his girls were growing up. It was far enough from the house for the men to get some quiet time yet close enough if he was needed in a hurry.

With the Fall River tracks complete, there was no need for the road to be used again, and Daniel's land would be hidden from the public again.

As a favor to Ryan and Daniel, Mick had documents drawn up to state that the road was private and would never be used by the railroad again.

With Thanksgiving approaching, Abby and the girls decided they wanted to go into town for a few items for the celebration. Ryan suggested that Abby and her sisters have a day out since Abby had been with the babies all those months.

Against her better judgment, Abby agreed.

"How bad could taking care of three little girls be?" Ryan said. "Besides, Mick and Pop are with me."

Abby looked at him. "Ryan, you and Mick and Pop are three babies watching my babies."

Daniel shot her back a look. "Now, look here, I did my fair share of watchin' you young'ns, and you all turned out fine."

She saw she'd hurt her father's feelings. "I'm sorry, Papa. It's not really you I'm worried about."

"I promise you no harm will come to them babies," he said.

She gave him a hug. "Papa, I know you love the girls."

Mick walked in the door, his arms filled with gifts. "Okay, Uncle Mick is here, and look what he's got."

Abby shook her head, but she couldn't help but smile. She loved Mick like a brother, and he was the babies' godfather, but with all the girls they had, they'd have to make a bigger bedroom for them or move to another house.

Jenny walked up to them and gave Mick a kiss on the cheek.

"Will you be this way when we have our children?"

Mick turned to Ryan and winked. "No, Ryan will since I'll have spent all my money on his girls."

Ryan smiled at his wife. "All right, ladies, it's time you all get on your coats and get ready to head for town."

Abby started to pull the wagon away, and she looked back at the three men holding babies in their arms and waving goodbye to them. It was a sweet sight.

Jenny patted Abby on the back. "It'll be all right, Abby. Come on, let's get into town, and we'll be back in no time."

Back at the house, Ryan was getting the bottles ready for the girls.

Mick walked into the kitchen with Annie in his arms. "How's the milk coming? Little Annie here is getting hungry."

"I have the same problem with Meghan. Sometimes, I wonder how Abby does it."

Mick smiled at him. "Women are good at this. It's built in. The minute the babies are born, they can handle their regular chores and more.

My sister had five kids all a year apart and still ran a restaurant back in Pennsylvania. It was really something to watch her be a mother and still run a business."

Ryan was impressed. "I was an only child. So were my folks."

About that time, Daniel wandered into the room. "Now, boys, I know this is all new to you, but if these little ladies don't eat soon, their ma will hear them."

Ryan grabbed the bottle from the hot water, but Daniel grabbed it from him.

"It's a good thing you got me here. Now, look here and learn somethin'." Daniel placed a few drops of milk on his arm to test how hot it was. "You don't want to burn their throat, do ya?" He proceeded to then give Meghan her milk. "Ain't nothin' to it."

He watched as both men tested the milk and then fed the babies.

# CHAPTER ELEVEN

In town, the girls were greeted by Father Cahill coming out of the church.

"Well, this is a pleasant surprise," he said. "And how are those lovely little girls?"

Abby smiled. "We left them home with the men. I hope the good Lord is watching over them, Father."

"Be assured, Abby, they have angels watching over them always. And what about you, Jenny? When are we going to see you married?"

"Oh Father, you know we're planning to marry next summer."

"Ah, yes. It's a wonderful time of the year."

"Father," Abby said. "If you're not going anywhere for Thanksgiving, we would be happy to have you join us."

The man looked at her, and for a moment, he thought of their mother. Molly McVinny had raised caring and compassionate children.

"That is very kind of you, Abby."

"Well, don't forget, Father. We'll be expecting you."

He smiled as he continued on his way, and the girls walked into the general store.

Mrs. Dixon, the owner of the store, greeted Abby. "It's so good to see you, dear. I was just telling the mister this morning that the last time we saw you and the girls was at their baptism. So what can I do for you girls today?"

"We left the girls home with the men today so they will understand how it is with three babies all crying at the same time."

Mrs. Dixon chuckled. "Why Abigail Lochlan, that is cruel, leaving those poor men to deal with those women, and you know they have them tied around their little fingers."

All four women laughed and joked about that. The sisters continued their shopping, going into the dress shop next door.

Later in the day, they started back home. The sky was turning a shade of gray and getting darker. This was precisely what Abby had feared: rain. Jenny looked at her sister and knew what she was thinking.

"It will be all right, Abby. We'll be home before the storm even hits here."

Looking at the sky from a window, Ryan noticed the clouds moving faster across the sky. The girls were asleep, which made Ryan wonder whether he should ride out and meet up with the girls so that he knew they were safe.

Abby was leading the horses when she felt a raindrop. She still hoped they could get home before the rain fell harder. "Jenny, get in the back, and you and Mary get under the tarp. You'll be out of the rain."

"We're not leaving you, Abby," Mary said.

"Don't be silly," Abby replied. "We don't all have to get wet."

"You don't have to be the one to get wet," Mary said. "After all, you have the babies to think about."

"Abby, we can take turns," Jenny said. "The house is still six miles away."

Ryan was pacing the floor and wondering where the girls were.

Mick noticed how worried he looked. "Something isn't all right, is it?"

"Mick, I've got to go out there and see where they are. It could be nothing, but I would feel better if I went and got them."

Mick put his hand on Ryan's shoulder. "Then go. Go bring our girls back home."

Ryan nodded to himself, got his hat, and headed out the door. Daniel came into the hall just as Ryan was heading out.

"I was wondering when he was goin' to go after them."

Mick turned to Daniel. "You knew all along what he was worried about?"

"Son, you don't know much about that boy, do you? He loves that gal of mine, and nothin' is gonna keep them apart."

A flash of lightning momentarily blinded the girls. A tree a few yards ahead of them fell to the ground with a heavy thud. It was on fire.

Abby slowed the wagon and sat down in the back under the tarp. Completely soaked to the skin, Abby prayed Ryan would come and find them.

The rain and wind pounded at Ryan as he continued to make his way down the trail. Hardly able to see a few feet ahead, he thought his eyes were playing tricks on him when he saw an image of a wagon on the side of the road.

The clap of thunder was followed by a bolt of lightning illuminating the path, and Ryan could see the wagon and the horse on the side of the road.

As he made his way to the wagon, he called out Abby's name.

Under the tarp, Abby thought she heard his voice but then thought it was just the wind. Once again, she heard her name and slowly lifted the tarp up to find Ryan standing in the rain.

"Nice evening for a ride isn't it? Mind if I join you?" Secretly, he was extremely relieved, but Ryan grinned as if he was the suavest fella in the world.

"The lightning... the tree... the—" Abby gasped.

"Well, I think we should get back home, where we can be nice and dry, where we can talk about this eventful day. Unless you'd rather stay here and talk under that tarp. Girls, what do you think?"

Jenny and Mary both chimed in. "Home, Ryan, please."

He winked at Abby as he tied his horse to the back of the wagon, then he climbed aboard.

Abby got out from under the tarp to sit at his side. Slowly, the wagon made its way down the mud-soaked road. Ryan looked at Abby, by his side. Even soaked to the skin and shivering, she still was beautiful. Abby looked back at him and felt his strength and warmth when he wrapped one arm around her, holding her close.

As the wagon turned a bend on the road leading to the house, the rain seemed to let up. Thunder sounded in the distance, and the lights from the house could be seen from where they were as the wagon moved on.

Mick was pacing on the porch before the wagon pulled up. He didn't see Jenny and Mary. "Did you forget the other girls in town, Abby?"

Jenny lifted the tarp and smiled. She gave Mick a big hug.

"We're here, Mick. Abby made us sit under this smelly tarp. She's been so cruel to us."

Abby glared at her sister. "That smelly tarp kept you out of both the wind and rain."

Mary shook her head at both of them. "It doesn't matter, does it? We're home now."

Mick helped the girls off the wagon, picking Jenny up first and lifting her off the wagon, and then Mary. Daniel came out of the house and breathed a sigh of relief, seeing that the girls had safely reached home.

"I knew Ryan would git everyone home."

Abby smiled at her father as she got off the wagon. "Thanks, Papa."

The rain seemed to have almost stopped, and Daniel put his arm around Abby. "You three had better get those wet clothes off and sit by the fire."

"I want to check in on the girls first."

Daniel took her hand. "Git out of those clothes first."

"You're right, Papa."

She turned back to Ryan. "Oh, can you two take the supplies off the wagon for us?"

Mick and Ryan looked at each other then together gracefully bowed and said, "Anything else, me lady?"

She made a face at them. "Go, both of you."

The weather turned cold, and winter was showing her bitter side. The chilly wind from the north made it impossible for anyone to stay out for any longer than a half hour, and even that was unbearable.

Both Ryan and Mick were busy chopping wood for the fireplaces to make sure the house was warm.

Abby and Jenny had gone to the attic to get Molly's old quilts, to nail against the windows to stop the frigid air from seeping through. Mary and Daniel took care of the girls by keeping them warm and happy.

The back door flew open, and Ryan and Mick came in along with a burst of wind. Daniel covered Molly with her blanket.

"Looks like it's building up out there," Daniel said. "Did ya lock the barn down?"

"Did that first, Pop, and made sure Maggie Mae was milked."

Daniel nodded in satisfaction and started to rock Molly.

Suddenly, Jenny came running into the kitchen. "Papa, Papa. It's Uncle Gideon! He's coming up the road."

Ryan and Mick looked at each other then at Daniel. Neither had ever heard of a Gideon. Daniel set Molly in her cradle and headed toward the front of the house.

"Best be I go and greet dear brother Gideon."

When Daniel was out of earshot, Ryan turned to Jenny. "Gideon?"

"He's Papa's younger brother. He took off years ago. I think I was about five at the time. Papa always said he was a bad seed. Wonder what he's doing back here. This can't be good."

Jenny picked up Molly and headed to the front of the house, where Mary and Abby were.

Daniel waited for the knock on the door then opened it. "Gideon," he said without much enthusiasm.

Gideon blinked back at his brother. "Is this the greeting a brother gives to his kin? Come on, Danny boy, give me a hug."

Daniel obliged, patting him on the back.

After pulling out of the embrace, Gideon looked around. "Where's my favorite gal? Molly! Molly, girl, where are you hiding?"

Wordlessly, Daniel stepped aside to let Gideon in.

"Molly, Molly, are you in the kitchen?"

Abby approached him when she saw that her pa wasn't setting him straight. "She's not here, Uncle Gideon. Mama passed a while ago."

The smile on Gideon face faded, and he stumbled to the nearest chair to sit. "Passed? Molly? It can't be true. She was a young woman. How did it happen?"

Daniel stood near him. "She was killed."

"Killed? Did you say killed?"

"I did."

Gideon stared at the floor then looked up and met Abby's eye.

"Abigail? You are Abigail, right?"

"Yes, Uncle Gideon. I'm Abby, and this is Jenny and Mary."

He looked around again. "Annie, where's Annie?"

"She was killed with Mama." Abby told him what had happened. At the news, he bowed his head and wept. When he looked up, the tears rolling down his cheeks tore at Abby's heart.

"But..." Gideon's lip quivered slightly. "Molly was like a sister to me."

Gideon was closer to Molly than to his own brother, who was nothing like him. The brothers rarely saw eye to eye. That was why

Gideon had left soon after the twins were born. And after fifteen years, he had returned.

Ryan came in and stood next to his wife.

"Uncle Gideon, this is my husband, Ryan Lochlan," Abby said.

Ryan extended his hand. "Pleased to meet you, sir."

He turned to Ryan. "Pleased to meet you, son. You're not from round here, are you?"

"No, sir. I'm from Ireland."

"Ireland, ya say. Is that up north?"

Abby smiled. "No, Uncle Gideon, it's across the ocean. It's another country."

Daniel looked at his brother incredulously. "Gideon, didn't you learn nothin' in school?"

"You know I never went past fifth grade, Daniel. When Pa died, I had to tend the farm. Heck, you and Jeb were gone already. I was the only one left at home."

Daniel had forgotten that chapter in his life.

"I left at eighteen," Daniel explained to Ryan. "Never got along with old Pa. I thought my brothers would care for the farm and my parents, but things didn't always go as planned. Years later, Jeb left and headed out west, never to be heard from again."

"I was the baby of the family," Gideon added. "Pa had been a hard man. I guess I don't blame my brothers for wanting to get away. God knows how Ma put up with him. When she died, I was the only one left, and I gave the farm to some nice folks and then traveled from place to place. The only family I had were my brothers, and though I didn't know were Jeb was, I know where to find Daniel."

Jenny handed Gideon a hot cup of coffee.

"Uncle Gideon, this might warm you up."

"Thank you, Jenny—am I right?"

"Yes, Uncle Gideon. I'm Jenny."

He turned back to Daniel. "I'm sorry for barging in on you, Daniel. I was just passing through when the wind started to build up, and..."

"You don't have to apologize, Uncle Gideon," Abby interrupted. "You're family, and you are staying with us for as long as you like."

He smiled at her. "You are Molly's daughter, all right. Just like her, you are." He turned to Ryan. "You know you're a lucky man, son."

"Oh, I know that. She's a special lady."

"That she be."

That evening, as the wind howled outside and the tree branches snapped and flew against the house, the family inside were enjoying a good meal in a warm home. Feeling nostalgic, Gideon reminisced about their childhood.

"Daniel, do you remember when Ma got so mad at us for going fishing on Sunday and not to Sunday service?"

"Ma always was on us for going to Sunday service."

"I remember Reverend Gideon always taught Sunday school and took us home after."

Abby looked up from her plate.

"*Reverend* Gideon?"

"Yes," Gideon replied. "He was our pastor back home."

"Were you named after him, Uncle Gideon?"

Both Daniel and Gideon were both silent, thinking about it for a moment. Somehow, that had never crossed Gideon's mind. When the reverend came to visit, he was only visiting his congregation members that could not attend church.

Then Gideon started to remember how townfolk would talk about him as though he was some unwanted child. True, he didn't look like his brothers or his parents, but there were men who didn't look like their siblings.

Abby saw that she'd opened a memory that should have stayed a memory. "Pie, Uncle Gideon?"

He was so lost in his thoughts that she asked him again. "Uncle Gideon, would you like some pie?"

"Oh, yes, thank you." He looked at his brother. "Do you think—"

Daniel cut him off. "Don't be thinking that. You know Ma was a good woman. Don't listen to what those old biddies back home thought."

As if on cue, the girls began to cry. Ryan, Mick, and Mary headed to the bedroom to get them. Gideon watched as Ryan handed Little Molly to Abby.

"Uncle Gideon, this is Molly," she said, bringing the baby close to him.

He looked at the adorable baby girl with the rosy cheeks. "Abby, she's a beauty. Your ma would have been so proud of you."

"Would you like to hold her?"

"Oh, no, Abby. I'm not clean, and I wouldn't want to—"

"Don't be silly. She's part McVinny, and we're indestructible." She placed Molly in his arms, and a smile came over her face. "See, I told you, and you were worried for nothing."

"I think she likes me." He looked up at Daniel. "It's been too many years. I'm tired of moving around."

"You want to come home, is that it?"

Daniel got up and walked over to the fireplace. He looked at the fire and thought of what his mother and Molly would say. After all, he was his little brother. He was kin.

He turned, and all in the room were looking at him.

"I have only one thing to say," Daniel said. "And that is: welcome home, Gideon."

Abby jumped up first and hugged her uncle. "Welcome home, Uncle Gideon."

# CHAPTER TWELVE

Later that evening, the wind calmed down, and snow covered everything outside the window. Daniel was sitting by the fire when Ryan slowly walked over to him.

"Everything okay, Pop?"

"I didn't have the heart to tell him."

"Tell him what, Pop?"

"Gideon ain't my true brother."

"True brother?"

"Mama, well she and the reverend were... well... Lord, I don't blame her. She took enough from my father, and..."

"Pop, it's okay. Gideon is your brother, and no one will ever say different. If they do, they'll deal with me."

The old man looked at him with gratitude. "Thank you, son. I had a feeling you would understand."

"It's really okay, Pop. We're all family: you, me, Mick, the girls, the babies, and now Gideon."

Daniel smiled and nodded.

Ryan got up and headed toward the bedroom, leaving Daniel by the fire.

The morning brought a new adventure with snowdrifts blanketing the way to the barn and the chairs on the porch completely covered in white. Looking out the front door, one couldn't imagine there was actually a road under all the snow.

Abby walked up to the door as her father was looking at the snow. "Oh, this should be fun."

She went to the back of the house to look at the other path to the barn.

Ryan came up behind her and gave her a hug. "I see we got a little snow."

Mick walked into the kitchen and looked at the both of them, standing at the open door.

"Excuse me, but do any of you realize it's freezing in here with the door open?"

"Yeah," Abby said. "We're trying to figure out how to go and milk Maggie Mae."

Jenny was next to make it down the stairs. "It's freezing down here. Is the..." She stopped as she saw the open door and everyone looking outside. "Okay, so we have a ton of snow out there. Are there any ideas on how to get to the barn?"

"Well, it seems the only thing you can do is shovel as you walk," Mick remarked.

Jenny made a face at him. "I don't want to upset you, Mick, but the shovel is out there by the barn."

Mick smiled at all three of them and grabbed his coat.

"It can't be that hard. Come on, I'll show ya."

He stepped off the porch, and immediately, he was waist-deep in snow. The three on the porch couldn't help but laugh uncontrollably as Mick tried to get back onto the porch.

"I thought you said it was easy, Mick." Daniel came out to the porch and shook his head. "You're not gonna get Maggie Mae milked this way."

"I'm trying, Pop," Mick said, "but this snow is a bit deep."

After they got snow, the days raced by quickly until Christmas was only a day away. Ryan and Mick cut down the biggest tree around and took it back to the house. After a few more trimmings, they were able to bring it inside to be set up and decorated.

The entire family was at church for the service as Father Cahill welcomed Gideon to the congregation and congratulated Mick and Jenny on their engagement. Everyone enjoyed a huge reception in the church hall.

Mrs. Dixon was handing out candy to the other children but couldn't resist going over to Abby and her girls. "My goodness, Abby. They are growing so. It's so good to see all of you in town."

"Thank you, Mrs. Dixon."

Abby's girls were still too young to understand what the holidays were about, but that didn't stop Mick from showering them with gifts. While the family was preparing for a new year, with the wedding of Jenny and Mick planned for the coming summer, Abby still wished her mom could be there with them. She would have been so excited with the upcoming wedding, not to mention being with the grandchildren. Abby often thought of Little Annie and what she would've looked like. She had always been a happy child.

"Little Annie and Mama..."

She closed her eyes, and at that moment, a gentle breeze touched her cheek, almost as soft as a mother's kiss. This was not the first time she had felt it. After Molly died, Abby had felt her mother with her during the important moments in her life, the times when she needed Molly the most.

"Oh Mama, if you're still here, I hope you're satisfied with how we turned out. I wish you could hold the babies, and I know if you were here, they would love you. You were right, Mama. You knew Ryan was the one I would marry even if I didn't. You always knew what was best. I hope I will be the same with my girls."

Suddenly, a strange feeling came over her. Abby called out to Jenny and then fainted.

Jenny rushed out to the porch and saw Abby slumped in the chair. "Papa! Uncle Gideon! Come quick—something happened to Abby."

Everyone rushed to the front porch. Daniel was the first to arrive and checked her pulse. "I need someone to go into town. I think she's fainted, but I would like to be sure." Daniel turned to Jenny. "Can you ride in and get the doctor?"

"I'll be back as soon as I can."

Daniel turned to Gideon. "Let's get her into bed. Mary, can you handle the girls for a bit until we get Abby taken care of?"

"Of course, Papa."

Ryan and Mick were coming back from town when Jenny rode past them.

"Jenny! Jenny, what's wrong?"

"It's Abby. She was sitting on the porch when she called my name and fainted. I'm going into town to get the doctor." She gave Mick a quick kiss and then continued into town.

Ryan and Mick rushed back to the house. They arrived to see Mary sitting with the girls on the porch. Ryan got off his horse and ran into the house.

In the bedroom, Ryan found Daniel applying compresses to Abby's forehead. Fortunately, Abby was awake and talking to her father.

Ryan breathed a sigh of relief and sat on the bed. "What happened?"

"I was just sitting on the porch and felt funny. The next thing I knew, I was here in the bedroom, and Papa and Uncle Gideon were by my side."

In town, Jenny rushed to Doc Bailey's office. She banged on the door but heard no answer. She banged again in desperation—still no answer.

As she continued banging, while quickly losing hope, Doc Bailey walked up to her.

"Is there a reason for the loud banging on my door, Miss McVinny?"

"Oh, Doc. You've got to come out to the house. Something has happened to Abby." Jenny quickly explained what had transpired earlier.

"Well let me get my carriage and my bag, and we'll head out to the house. Has she ever had this before?"

"No, Doc."

Abby was sitting up when Jenny arrived with Doc Bailey.

"All right," said Doc Bailey, "I need some room to work here, so I need everyone but Abby out of the room."

Everyone left for the dining room, where Mary was feeding the girls. In the bedroom, Doc Bailey asked Abby the usual questions.

"So you're telling me that you were on the porch, and you felt funny and fainted."

"Yes, that's what happened."

He continued the examination, and after about fifteen minutes, he was done.

"Doc, what is the problem?" Abby asked.

"Mrs. Lochlan, you'll be fine." The doctor smiled.

"What happened?"

"My dear lady, you're going to have a baby."

"A baby, Doc Bailey! I already have a set of triplets. I don't think I can go through that again."

"Well, Mrs. Lochlan, you're going to have a baby, and it will be end of summer."

Abby was in too much shock to answer.

A knock came from the door.

"Come in," Doc Bailey called.

Ryan walked in and rushed to his wife's side. "Doc, is everything okay?"

"Mr. Lochlan, I'll tell you like I just told your wife. She's going to have a baby."

Ryan digested the news. He was relieved that Abby was fine but a little taken aback. He nodded. "If you'll excuse me, Doc, the family has been waiting out there, and I want to put their minds at ease."

"Of course, by all means tell them."

"Please tell Papa to come in," Abby requested.

Ryan left and, on his way out, told Daniel she wanted to see him before breaking the news to the others.

Daniel went into the bedroom and smiled at his daughter.

"Feeling better, Abby? You gave us all quite a scare."

# Chapter Thirteen

For the next few months, Abby observed her body growing again. With Jenny's wedding only two months away, Abby found it harder and harder to move around.

Mary found her on the floor. Abby had been trying to pick up the girls' toys and couldn't get back up. Mary had been sitting in the living room, reading a book, when it happened.

"Ryan! Papa! I need you both here now," Mary called.

Daniel came running in. "What's wrong, Abby?"

"The baby—it's coming."

Ryan spun around to find Mick. "We need Doc Bailey. Abby's having the baby." He grabbed

Jenny and Mary. "Get the babies. Keep them busy. I—"

"Ryan, go to Abby. We'll handle the rest," Jenny said.

He raced back to the bedroom, where Abby was carrying on. "This baby isn't due yet. Jenny's wedding is in three weeks. I don't have time for all this."

Ryan blinked at her. "You make the time. The doc is on his way. You did it without a doctor last time. Come on, Abby, you can do it."

He took her hand in his. She felt a contraction and squeezed his hand so hard she almost broke it. He didn't say a word but looked into her eyes. He didn't know how much time passed as he held her hand, nor did it matter. He was there for her, and that was all that mattered to him.

A light tap came from the door. Doc Bailey came in the room. "Well, it seems that this baby wants to come out for the wedding."

Abby smiled, but that faded when she had another contraction.

"That one was a strong one, wasn't it?" the doc asked.

She just nodded. She was still holding Ryan's hand when the pain returned again.

The doctor turned to Ryan. "Lochlan, I need Jenny in here."

"What's wrong, Doc?"

"Oh, there's nothing wrong. It's just I need Jenny to help Abby have twins."

Ryan's jaw dropped. Wordlessly, he closed it. He did as he was told and found Jenny, who was in the kitchen boiling water. "Jenny, the doctor wants you in the room. Seems Abby is having twins."

"Twins. Oh, Lord." She rushed into the bedroom.

For the next eight hours, the door was closed, and no one went in or out. Mary kept the coffee coming, and Daniel and Gideon kept the girls busy. Mick and Ryan paced the floor and waited to hear the sound of a baby's cry.

They were going into the eighth hour when they finally heard a baby's wail.

Mick patted Ryan's shoulder as they waited for the second cry. After a few more minutes, they heard it.

Jenny came out and smiled at Ryan. "You have two handsome sons."

Ryan just stood there, speechless. The girls had just started walking, and he had two more babies.

He rubbed his face and then went in.

A minute later, Ryan and Jenny came out of the room, holding the newest additions to the Lochlan family. Ryan took the boy in his arms over to Daniel.

"Pop, I'd like you to meet Daniel Gideon."

Both Daniel and Gideon smiled and cooed at the baby.

Jenny brought the second boy over to Mick and Mary. "And this is Thomas Michael Lochlan."

"They named him after me?" Mick exclaimed.

"Well, the Michael is. The Thomas is for Ryan's dad."

In the bedroom, Doc Bailey was tired, but not as tired as Abby.

"So how do you feel now, Mrs. Lochlan?" he asked.

"Exhausted, Doc."

"Well, I'm going to let you rest a bit. You just get some rest and don't get up too soon. A lot of people are here to help you."

As he left the room, he noticed she was already starting to doze off. He closed the door behind him and joined everyone in the living room.

Ryan offered to pay him. "What do I owe you, Doc?"

"I'd say two dollars, and promise that young lady in there gets some rest. Lord knows, five kids in three years—it takes a lot out of a woman."

"I promise, Doc."

Ryan went back into the bedroom to see his wife, leaving Daniel busy with little Danny.

He looked down at her as he moved closer. She looked beautiful, even after hours of intensive labor.

She opened her eyes and smiled up at him. "Hi."

"Hi, yourself," Ryan said.

"The babies..."

"They're being taken care of, along with the girls. We're gonna need a bigger house or stop having children." He sat down beside her and took her hand. "Did anyone ever tell you how beautiful you are?"

"Not in a while. You see, my husband is a very busy man."

"Then he is a foolish man, for you should be told how beautiful you are every day." He kissed her hand and smiled at her.

Moments like those needed no words. She knew of the love he had for her, and he knew that he had truly found that perfect soul whom he wanted to spend the rest of his days with.

Life continued to be even more hectic at the McVinny farm with the twins, but with Jenny and Mick's wedding happening, not even the birth of twin boys was going to change the plans of the McVinny women, especially when it came to having a good time. Since it was hard for Abby to get around, Jenny and Mick suggested that the wedding be held at the home.

Abby wouldn't hear of it. "You're getting married in the church, and I don't want to hear another word."

"Don't be silly. We can still have Father Cahill come," said Jenny.

"Don't you think I'm letting a sister of mine not get married in a church."

"Abby, this is not your decision. It's my wedding, and I will get married wherever I want."

"All right, as you want."

Jenny saw that she had upset her. "Abby, I love you and would do anything you asked, but this is one thing I will not change. I want my sister at my wedding—and my nieces and nephews—so the only way that will happen is to have the ceremony here."

The big day had come. Jenny was wearing a dress Mick had purchased for her in Boston, and Mrs. Dixon had altered it to fit her. Jenny was about to become Mrs. Mick Dawson, and yes, she was getting married at the house so her sister could attend.

Daniel was watching his girls grow up and marry and leave him right before his eyes. He walked into the room as Jenny put the last touches on her hair. "You look beautiful, Jenny."

"Thanks, Papa."

"I can't believe my girls are all grown up. You won't be needing your pa anymore."

Jenny put her arms around him. "Now, Papa, you know that's not true. We'll always need you, and don't you ever think we don't."

He gave her a kiss on the cheek, and they headed down the stairs to go outside.

As the ceremony was finishing, a white dove flew by. Abby knew it was from her mom. She smiled as she watched it fly. "Bye, Mama," she whispered.

The reception was filled with music and food. Even Abby surprised herself by dancing with her husband, but everyone told her not to push herself.

After they were tired out by all the fun, the family sent Jenny and Mick on their honeymoon.

Jenny gave Abby one more hug before boarding the ship. "Thanks so much, Abby. Now promise you'll get more rest when I'm gone."

"I promise. Now get on the boat."

Jenny looked at her father as he waved to her. Oh, how she was gonna miss them.

Everyone on the dock waved goodbye as their cruise ship headed for New York.

As they drove back to the house, Abby was realizing that the family she'd grown up with was changing. Soon, Jenny would be having her own children. It wouldn't be long before Mary found a young man, and she'd be going off and getting married.

There she was with five children. Who would have thought? Seemed like it wasn't so long ago when Abby and her sisters were wondering if their papa would ever let them meet a fella.

She still remembered the first time she'd seen Ryan. She opened the door to find the handsomest man she had ever seen in her life, and he left her speechless. She could only smile since somehow she couldn't utter a word. All she could think of was how silly he must have thought she was.

Who would've thought they would have five children together? She thought about them for a moment and smiled to herself.

She was married to a man who loved her with his heart and soul. Looking over at Ryan, she wondered whether he ever thought back in his Ireland that he would come to America and end up on a little farm in Massachusetts with a wife and five children.

Ryan looked at his wife and remembered it was Mick who'd first noticed that he had fallen in love with her. The times he would go out to the farmhouse for any reason because seeing her was the highlight of his day, those stolen glances he remembered. Her smile always lit up his life. He'd keep those smiles in his memory until the next time he saw her. He was drawn to her like a moth drawn to a flame, and her magic was love—the ever-after love that nothing would ever take from them.

At night, Abby watched the full moon as clouds seemed to race across it. Her mother would say they were the spirits of those who had passed on going home to the campfires in the sky. Molly had a story for everything.

Molly had been a natural-born storyteller. She could make her girls believe they were descendants of the Shawnee tribe and that Molly was the granddaughter of one of their chiefs.

Only later did Abby learn that Molly's story came from the mission school Molly had been raised in. Molly had been orphaned at the age of six when her parents died in a fire. She remembered only her father getting her out of the house and going back to get her mother when the roof caved in, trapping them both in there. And so Molly Payton was placed in the mission-school orphanage. The only things she had left were her memories and her name. She did well at the mission school, graduated in the top ten of her class, and became a teacher.

Teaching was the one thing she loved the most until Daniel McVinny walked into her life. He was like no other man she had ever met. Against everyone's advice, she allowed him to court her and soon realized his dreams were not much different from hers. A home and a person to share life with were all they needed. In Daniel, Molly found a love that would last a lifetime, a love that would reach out and hold on to her heart until their days on earth were done... and longer.

That was what Molly Payton was: a woman, a wife, a mother, and more. She instilled in her girls those same qualities, and as Abby looked back on her mother, she realized that each of them was like Molly in certain ways.

Ryan walked up behind her and put his arms around her waist. He looked up at the moon. "Wishing on that old gypsy moon, are ye?"

She turned and looked at him. "Gypsy moon?"

"Sure, my mother told me the story. Back before there was an Ireland, a band of Celtic warriors landed on a land that they called Galicia. It's in Spain. Well, these warriors conquered this land for years, and from the tallest peak in Galicia, they noticed a land across the sea. They sent warriors to this new land across the ocean and settled there, calling it Ireland. For those who stayed in Galicia, they kept the traditions and culture of their tribe. They became what many call gypsies, and their bagpipes still flow across the mountains and valleys with their haunting melodies. At night, when the moon is full, like it is now, you can see the gypsies dancing in the moonlight, going back home to Galicia."

Abby laughed lightly. "It's true—you Irish are truly full of blarney."

"'Tis a true story. Me mother told me herself, and her descendants were part of those warriors."

Abby looked at him and then back at the moon. "Ya know, it does look like someone is dancing in the moonlight."

"Would you care to dance, my lady?"

She took his hand. "Another thing, why did Mick always call you Lancelot?"

"Well, Mick knew I had fallen in love with a fair maiden even before I did. He said I was your knight in shining armor, Sir Lancelot, fighting for his lady fair."

"And were you fighting for your lady?"

He held her closer. "I won her, did I not, her and her kingdom? And together they will live happily ever after."

"And we will live happily ever after because we are the gypsies dancing in the moonlight." She looked into his eyes, and for those moments in time, nothing mattered because, for them, time stood still.

# CHAPTER FOURTEEN

Seven years had passed.

Abby and Ryan still lived on the farm, along with Uncle Gideon. Daniel had gone to join his beloved Molly, who he always said was waiting there for him.

Though they felt the sorrow of not having him with them, they also knew he missed his Molly and wanted to be with her.

The girls had sadly buried their father beside Molly and Annie, as he had wished. Then they had the details of his estate that needed to be dealt with. The local attorney, Carter L. Duffy, who had known Daniel for years, was given the duty of reading the will. On a warm Saturday afternoon a week after Daniel's passing, the girls and Gideon sat at the dining-room table.

Mr. Duffy read the will. After the usual formalities, he came to the shares:

"I hereby leave to my daughter Abigail and her husband the farm with the stipulation that my brother Gideon be allowed to live there for the rest of his days.

"To my daughter Jennifer and her husband Mick, I leave the sum of fifty thousand dollars. That was the price of the coal rights that I received when I sold the land to the railroad with the stipulation that I and my heirs would get a percentage.

"To my youngest Mary, I leave you fifty thousand dollars as your half of the share your sister has."

Mr. Duffy folded the paper back up. "Well, it appears that Daniel had everything taken care of before he departed."

Jenny turned to Abby. "Seems he only gave you the farm. Abby, I hope you're not disappointed."

"No, not at all. I always loved the farm."

Abby found her sister's remark a bit odd. Since her move to New York, Jenny had changed drastically. She never had time for her family anymore but was always in the society pages. Mary, on the other hand, was still the shy young girl who had lost her twin so long before. She had gone to stay with Jenny and Mick for a few weeks but came back, not wanting to return again.

Three months after the reading of the will, Abby found out why.

When the society pages heard that Jenny was returning to Fall River, an entourage of press followed her on the ship to write about it. She sent a wire to Abby to have the house presentable and Uncle Gideon in town so the press wouldn't see him. She wanted to avoid any embarrassment.

Abby looked at the wire and shook her head. "She's gone too much now. If she's embarrassed at us, she need not stop here. And Mick, I'm surprised at him letting her do this."

Ryan looked at her. "Abby, Mick and Jenny are not together anymore. He got fed up with her lifestyle and moved out."

"Oh Ryan, why didn't you tell me?"

"He moved back to Pennsylvania and took Holly with him."

"My little niece. Oh... that sister of mine!"

"I want you to behave yourself and act like a lady when she's here," Ryan said.

"But why is she coming here, Ryan?"

"You'll see."

Moments later, the sound of wagons coming up the road signaled Jenny's arrival. Ryan led Abby to the porch as Jenny waved at them. The driver helped her down, and she walked up to her sister and gave her a kiss on the cheek. "It's so good to see you, Abigail."

She smiled at Ryan. "It's so good to see you also. Are the children around? I've gotten some gifts for them."

"No, they are in school today," Abby said. "By the way, how is Holly?"

"She lives with her aunt in Pennsylvania. With me traveling all the time, it's no life for her."

Ryan looked at her strangely but thought better than to comment on her remark. "Would you care to come in?"

She gave him a smile and walked into the house. The press wanted to follow, but Abby stopped them.

"I'm sorry, but my home is not for display, and I would like to spend some private time with my sister. I'm sure you all can understand."

One of the reporters got rather snippy. "Hey, what's the story here? Jenny said we would be able to follow her all over. We want to see the grave of her mother, the Indian princess."

"Excuse me! Our mother was not an Indian princess."

Jenny came back outside when she heard the argument. "Oh Abby, you remember the story Mama told us about the moon."

"Yes and that's all it was, Jenny, a story. Mama's name was Molly Payton. Her parents died in a fire, and they were Leo and Margaret Payton. I don't know what you are telling these people, but I am not having my house put on some sort of display for your lies."

"How dare you!" Jenny cried. "You not only insult me but you call me a liar!"

"I don't appreciate you coming here and turning our home and our family into part of your story. You were never like this Jenny. Why, when is the last time you saw your daughter?"

"That's none of your business."

Abby walked out of the room and left Jenny alone.

After Jenny went back to New York, Mick sent a wire to Ryan, telling them that Jenny had filed for a divorce and was heading to England. The two sisters never spoke again.

When Ryan told Abby, she just looked out the window. "I'm glad Papa is gone. This would have killed him. To think she would do this. She just picked up and left her family like this. I doubt even Mama would forgive her for this."

"Whatever she's done, Mick and Holly are still family."

"Of course they are. What makes you think they're not?"

"Well, just so you know, I've asked them to come to visit with us for a few days. This way, Holly can see the girls, and Mick can have time to figure out what he plans to do."

"He can stay here as long as he needs. Holly can share the room with the girls, just until we can get the upstairs done and have the bedrooms there. We were thinking on extending the house anyhow. We can always use more bedrooms. The girls, Holly, Mary, Ryan, and the twins could have upstairs, Gideon can have Papa's old room, and we have ours."

Ryan put his arms around her and held her close.

"You know, that's why I love you, Abby. Don't ever change. I love you just the way you are."

She looked up at him and smiled.

The house was enlarged to accommodate the big family, and they even added a porch with a balcony overlooking Molly's roses down below. That way, she had enough bedrooms for everyone and a few guest rooms.

# CHAPTER FIFTEEN

A few years later, the brewing talk of war finally came to a head, along with the firing of Fort Sumter. When Ryan and Mick first started talking about it, Abby began to worry. Sitting at the supper table, both men and Uncle Gideon were engrossed in the subject when Ryan noticed his wife getting upset.

"Something wrong, Abby?" he asked.

"Ryan Lochlan, how can you and Mick sit here and talk about nothing but this dang war."

"But Abby—"

She turned to Mick next. "And you're no better. The idea of both of you planning to go off and play soldier, why it's... it's..."

"It's what, Abby?"

Uncle Gideon was at the table watching Ryan as he tried to get out of this one. "If it gets you upset, we won't talk about it."

"I want your promise that you won't go."

Ryan and Mick both looked at her with innocent looks on their faces.

"Us? I don't think so, Abby," Ryan said. "See, Mick and I, well, we're too old."

Mick turned to him. "Speak for yourself, there. I'm still in my prime."

Abby pointed a finger at him. "And with a young daughter, and don't forget that."

They smiled and promised nothing more would be said at the supper table. Gideon kept eating his supper, knowing that if it wasn't for Abby, Ryan would be out the door. Every day, men were volunteering for the army: young, old, some not even shaving yet. All wanted to be in those fancy uniforms and to become heroes.

After some time, Mary found a gentleman who was interested in her and she in him. He lived in town with his mother, who did laundry for people. Tim McIntire was a likable boy. He did seem to make the glow come back to her face and the sparkle to her eyes after the tragedy of losing her twin sister. Though Tim and Mary had only been together a short time, Abby had a feeling it could be serious.

Then one night, Mary came home in tears. She rushed up the stairs to her room, where she could cry alone into her pillow.

Abby looked at Ryan and then Gideon.

Gideon spoke first. "Better go tend to her, Abby. We've got the kids handled down here."

"Thanks, Uncle Gideon."

When she got up to Mary's room, she slowly opened the door. Mary was crying, and Abby could only conclude that she and Tim had had a disagreement. She walked over to her sister and sat beside her on the bed.

"Mary, what's wrong?" She lifted her sister's head and dried her tears with the back of her hand.

"It's Tim. He's got it in his head that he has to join the army, and... oh Abby, he says he's going and there's nothing that will change his mind."

Abby put her arms around her. The tears turned into sobs, and Mary felt as if her world was once again a deep void.

Abby tried to soothe her. "There, there. Don't worry. He'll probably think it over and realize he was wrong and will be here tomorrow, asking you to forgive him."

Mary looked at her sister with her sad eyes. "Do you think, Abby?"

"Maybe. We'll just have to see. Come on, let's go downstairs."

"Oh, I don't think so. I think I'll stay up here till morning."

Abby left her sister's room and went back down the stairs. Ryan looked at her expectantly, but she slowly shook her head. It wasn't until later that evening when they were sitting on the porch that Abby told Ryan what happened with Mary.

"That's a shame," Ryan said. "I really thought she had found someone."

"Mary's always kept to herself, ever since Little Annie passed. I tried to get her out of her shell, but... I was so sure that this boy was the one."

Ryan sighed. He took her hand in his, which cheered her up a little.

"Ryan, I'm so glad Papa ran you off the property that day."

"You are? Why do you say that?"

"Well, if he hadn't done that, you wouldn't have come back the next day, and I would've never met you."

He took her hand up to his lips and gently kissed it. "You know, if he had shot me, we'd never have met, either."

"Papa would have never shot you. Heck, the gun wasn't loaded."

He tilted his head at her in surprise. "Never loaded?"

"He'd had it hanging on the mantel for years. Didn't even know where the bullets were."

She started laughing and Ryan joined her.

"You mean," Ryan said, "when you had that gun aimed at those two who tried to–"

"No, I had the bullets in it then. I wasn't taking any more chances after Mama and Annie were killed."

He shook his head in surprise at her.

"Woman, you amaze me at times."

She only smiled at him. "Do I really? Is that a good thing or a bad thing?"

The following afternoon, Abby went out to the porch to tell Uncle Gideon supper was ready. She found him sitting on the chair.

She'd gotten close to him ever since his return. She had grown fond of him, and he was wonderful with the children.

"Uncle Gideon, it's time for supper. Uncle Gideon?"

She gently touched his shoulder, and the man slumped over.

"Ryan! Ryan!"

Ryan and Mick rushed outside when they heard her. Abby stood there, sobbing. Ryan looked over her shoulder and saw Gideon slumped over.

He shook his head at Mick. "Get her inside. I'll take care of Uncle Gideon."

At Uncle Gideon's somber ceremony, Ryan did the readings over the grave. Mick held Mary and Abby's shoulders. After the service, they all went inside.

When the children were in bed that evening, they talked about Gideon. Mary had only gotten to know Gideon as an adult since he'd left when she and Annie were just born. Abby recalled that he was the first one who taught her how to ride. He had a flaxen chestnut stallion, and he was just about the biggest horse Abby had ever seen. Oh, how she loved that horse! She would be at the corral each morning with a handful of carrots for her new friend. Molly had been a bit worried about putting her on such a big horse, but Abby wasn't afraid, and she knew Blaze would never hurt her.

Abby quickly got comfortable with the horse. She considered Blaze a best friend. For three years, Abby had freedom with Blaze, and then one day Uncle Gideon left, and so did a little girl's dreams.

Ryan sat near his wife as she continued her story.

"Uncle Gideon was the uncle everyone wanted and never got. It was hard to imagine that he and Papa were brothers. They were so different. But Mama, she always had a smile and kind words for him. And Gideon almost felt a special brother-sister bond with Molly."

Mary sat there in rapture, like a child hearing the story of Santa Claus. "Abby, why did he leave?"

"I really don't know. I mean, I was young, about six when he left. You and Annie had just been born a few months before that."

"Bet it was Papa. You know how he wanted things his own way. I heard Mama say to him one day that no one ever came to visit us because Papa didn't like visitors."

Abby looked out the window across the yard. Under the tree, the family had been laid. Molly had loved that tree. Ryan and Mick had cleared it out after Mama and Annie passed and fenced it all in. It felt as if they were all together there and still close to all of them still on earth. Abby always found it comforting to go there and talk to them as if they were there.

Ryan looked at his wife and touched her arm. "You all right, Abby?"

She turned and smiled at him. "Yeah, I'm just thinking of them and how I miss them."

He put his arm around her and drew her close. "It's been a rough day. Ready to turn in?"

She nodded, and they both got up from the sofa. "We're gonna hit the hay. See you both tomorrow."

Both Mick and Mary said goodnight.

Mary looked at Mick. "Can I get you some more coffee?"

"No, I'm fine. I should be heading up to bed also. Can I help you with anything here?"

"I was just going to take the cups into the kitchen. It's not that heavy."

He took the tray from her. "I know it's not heavy and you're a strong girl, but I'm taking it to the kitchen for you."

She gave him a quizzical look and placed her hands on her hips.

Mick ignored that. "Now, open the door, Mary."

She opened the door and followed him into the kitchen. He set the tray on the table, and Mary started to pump water into the sink.

"I thought you said you were just going to take them into the kitchen," Mick said.

"Well, at least it would be a good idea to have them soak overnight."

He looked at her carefully. She was not telling him something.

"Is there something wrong, Mary?" he asked.

She blinked back. "Wrong? No, nothing's wrong."

She stepped away from the sink and started for the door, but Mick gently grabbed her arm and turned her to face him.

"There is something wrong," he said. "What is it?"

"There's nothing wrong," she insisted.

"Mary, you were never a good liar. Have I done something to offend you?"

She looked into his eyes. She wanted to say so much to him, but she couldn't. It would be so wrong.

"You could never offend me, Mick. Why, you and Ryan are my big brothers, always watching out for me."

He shook his head. "And that's how you see me? As a big brother?"

She scrutinized his hurt expression.

"Is there something I should be seeing?" she asked.

He gently moved closer and kissed her on the cheek. "Mary, I want to be more than a big brother to you."

She froze but found the strength to turn, walk out the door, and run upstairs.

# CHAPTER SIXTEEN

Mary's flight was not missed by Abby, who had heard something and got up to see what the noise was. She walked into the hall as Mick was coming out of the kitchen.

He was about to go up the stairs when he accosted Abby. "I suppose you want an explanation about—"

"Mick, I love you like a brother, and I also love my baby sister. I want to know what you said to her to make her run up the stairs."

"Isn't it obvious, Abby? I love her! I have for quite a while now."

At first, she didn't know what to say.

"I see," Abby said slowly, "and when did you plan on telling us?"

"I haven't even told her. I don't know when or how it happened. I just looked at her one day, and it hit me."

"I see," Abby said again. "Well, how does Mary feel?"

"I'm not sure. I think she's confused."

"Maybe I should talk with her."

Upon hearing all the talking outside his bedroom, Ryan came out the door. "Here I am, coming out the door of my bedroom, and I find my wife and my best friend talking in the hall. What could this mean, I ask?"

"Oh hush, Ryan," Abby said crossly.

Both men looked at Abby in surprise.

"Mick, would you explain what's going on?" Ryan asked.

"It's simple. I'm in love with Mary."

"Well, of course you're in love with Mary," Ryan said in a joking tone. "You are talking about our Mary, right?"

Mick nodded.

"What are you thinking? She's only sixteen!"

"I'm aware of that, Ryan. I also know she is Abby's baby sister. But you both know I am a man of honor and really do love her and would be a good husband to her."

At that point, Abby felt the kitchen would be the best place to talk and pushed them both in.

She addressed Ryan. "Now, since both of you have known each other for a long time and since you introduced him to Jenny, is there any reason that you would not want him to marry Mary? Should she agree, that is."

"Abby, this is not the time or—"

"A simple answer to the question," Abby demanded of her husband.

"What about Holly?"

"What about Holly? Jenny has been out of her life for the past three years. Do you really think it's going to affect her either way?"

Just as Ryan was about to give his answer, Mary walked into the room. "I suppose everyone has the right to give their opinion on what is right and what is wrong and what is for my best, but I think I should be the one to give my opinion."

Abby looked at her sister with curiosity.

Mary continued, "I have been going over this for the past few weeks. I was tormented with the thought that I had feelings for my sister's husband and it was wrong. At Uncle Gideon's funeral, Mick had his arm on my shoulder, and I felt so protected. Still, he was my sister's husband. I didn't want to break up our family. It was Mick who listened to me when I found out Tim had gone off to war. But still, the one thing going through my head was he was my sister's husband."

Abby began to understand Mary's dilemma. "Mary, you have one detail wrong. Mick is not your sister's husband. They are divorced, and he is free to marry whomever he wants."

Ryan chimed in. "No one can say a word if you want to marry him. You are sixteen now and can marry."

With wide eyes, Mary looked from Abby to Ryan. "Are you trying to get rid of me?"

Abby laughed. "Never. All we are saying, honey, is we want you to be happy."

Mary turned to Mick. "Is that what you want? Me to be happy, whether or not I married you?"

He walked over to her and took her hand. "Mary, whatever you decide. As long as you are happy, I will be happy."

Ryan grabbed Abby's arm and slowly pushed her out the door, leaving Mick and Mary alone.

Once back in their room, she glared at Ryan. "What did you do that for?"

"I think they needed some privacy, don't you?"

"Do you think it's a good idea?"

He looked at her and smiled as he took her in his arms.

"Don't worry. It's Mick, not some young boy from town. Besides, he would have done the same for me. And I would like some privacy with my wife."

The morning rose with new promises. Mary and Mick had spent the whole night talking and coming to an agreement about their relationship.

Mary had finished making breakfast when Abby and Ryan came into the kitchen.

"Didn't we leave you two here? Didn't you go to bed at all?" Abby asked.

"Don't answer that until I have my coffee," Ryan said.

Mary poured him a coffee as he sat at the kitchen table. He looked from Mary to Mick and took a sip of his coffee.

"Okay, I'm ready. Wait... Is Abby going to be upset about this?"

"Well, I know you and Abby want what's best for me," Mary said. "So we've decided to wait a year, and then if we still feel the same, we'd like your blessing to marry."

Ryan was wondering whether to get Abby when she appeared. Abby had heard the conversation as she was walking in the door.

"I'll accept those terms," she said. "And I feel you both came to a good solution on this matter." She looked at Mary. "Are you sure this is what you want?"

"Yes," she said. "This way, there will be no mistakes."

"I don't have to tell you I'm happy and sad about this."

"Sad, Abby?"

"Well, I've had you with me all your life, and you were more than a baby sister." She turned to Mick. "Promise me you won't take her far away from me?"

"She's still gonna be with you for another year, and I promise she'll always be close enough. I couldn't take you two away from each other."

Abby smiled, somewhat satisfied with that answer.

Ryan broke the silence. "Well, I'm glad everyone is fine with this, but I would like to have some breakfast if neither of you would mind."

"Coming right up," Mary said cheerfully.

But the sound of horses coming up the road brought Ryan, Mick, and the girls to the front of the house.

Ryan looked at the others. "What could that be?"

# CHAPTER SEVENTEEN

A platoon of Union soldiers came up the road. They headed up the drive and came to a full stop at the foot of the porch steps. The captain in charge tipped his hat to the ladies and looked at Mick.

"Mr. Dawson, I am Captain Travis Kennedy. I have been given these orders by the President of the United States to seek your help in keeping the dock at Fall River safe from the Confederates. Here are your orders, sir."

He took a folded piece of paper from inside his shirt and handed it to Mick.

"Why me?" Mick asked. "I mean, there are other men who worked on the crew and know the line as well as I do."

"Because, Mr. Dawson, you were in charge of the security at the time. The President needs men he can trust. He also hopes you can persuade Mr. Lochlan to join you on this mission."

Abby looked at Ryan. "You can't—"

"Abby, it's not that far, and we have to do our part." He turned back to the captain. "Would you care to stop for some coffee and have your men relax a bit?"

"Thank you. Thank you very much." He dismounted and ordered the men to go in. Abby smiled at the captain.

"Captain Kennedy, forgive my manners. Please have your men sit wherever they like. I'll have coffee brought out to them."

He tipped his hat to her. "Thank you again, ma'am."

He followed them inside, where he saw the children and Mary at the table.

Abby introduced the family. "Captain Kennedy, these are my children, Molly, Annie, Meghan, Daniel, and Thomas and my niece Holly. This is my sister Mary."

He nodded to them.

"Mary, can we have some coffee for the captain's men outside?" Abby said. She turned back to Captain Kennedy. "Do sit down, Captain."

The captain did so and looked at Mick. "Well, Mr. Dawson, do we have an answer?"

Mick looked at Ryan then Abby. Ryan nodded.

"Tell the President Mr. Lochlan and I will take the assignment as long as it keeps us here in Fall River," Mick said.

Captain Kennedy smiled at them. "I'm sure I can confirm with the President that your assignment is only to be in Fall River."

Abby said a silent prayer for that. "Captain, do you think you have time for breakfast? We have plenty, and I'm sure your men would be happy to have a home-cooked meal."

"Thank you, Mrs. Lochlan, but we only have time to deliver our orders and leave." He looked at Mick. "Your office will be at the old railroad-line office so as not to cause any suspicion on anyone's part. Your cover will be that you are working for the railroad, keeping the docks open. I'll expect you there tomorrow. Oh yes, one more thing: you'll be assigned a telegrapher to handle all correspondence to and from Washington."

"Okay," Mick said.

The captain got up to leave. "Mrs. Lochlan, it was a pleasure, and thank you for your hospitality."

"You're welcome, Captain."

Mick and Ryan followed him out the door and watched them mount and ride off.

"Well, Ryan, it looks like we're back in the railroad business," Mick said.

"Guess we'd better go down and check things out. Could be some squatters on the land after all this time."

"I'll go tell Abby." Mick walked inside as Mary was starting to pick up the cups out on the porch. "Mary, you're not upset, are you?" he asked.

"Why would I be?" she asked. "You wanted to join up from the first day. You're not the first man who's left me for this dang war."

"Mary, it's not like that."

"It's not? Then you tell me—what is it, Mick? You said you loved me, that you'd never hurt me. Well you're doing that right now."

"Mary, it's just down the road. You can't—"

"And what happens when the Rebs come up the road and into our front yard?"

He started walking toward her, but she moved away.

"I really don't want to see you right now, Mick. Just leave me alone." She walked in the house and up the stairs as Abby and Ryan were coming out.

"What's wrong with Mary?" Abby asked.

"Seems your sister doesn't like my agreeing with the assignment," Mick replied.

"Doesn't she realize you are only going to be down the road? Let me go and talk to her."

"Not to hurt your feelings," Mick said, "but I think it's best to leave her alone for a while."

"Mick's right, Abby," Ryan chimed in. "Mary gets into one of her moods, and she'll crawl into that shell again."

She knew he was right.

"But Ryan, why don't you try?" Mick suggested. "After all, both she and Annie adored you. Maybe it will make a difference coming from you."

Ryan thought about it. "Okay, I'll talk to her. I'm not promising anything."

He headed upstairs toward Mary's door, and as he approached, he heard her sobbing. He lightly tapped on the door. "Mary, can I come in?"

"I'm not in the mood, Ryan."

"Mary, I just wanted to make sure you're all right, nothing more."

She opened the door and slowly stepped away so Ryan could enter. She sat on her bed, looking at the floor.

"We were all worried about you," Ryan said.

"I know. It was silly of me to carry on this way."

"Now, you have concerns, and Mick just started, but we really are only down the road. You can come and see us every day."

She looked up at Ryan. He was still that knight in shining armor. "I know. It's just—"

"Mary, Mick loves you, and nothing will change that."

"But—"

He smiled at her. "I think you should go and talk to Mick. I think he's on the porch up here."

She got up from the bed and kissed Ryan on the cheek before heading out the door.

Ryan smiled and silently thanked himself. "You still have it, Ryan boy."

He made his way downstairs to the living room, where Abby was getting ready to read a story to the children.

She raised her head, meeting his eyes and smiling. "All go well?"

As he sat down beside Molly, she handed her father the book. "Papa, would you read us the story?"

As the children gathered closer, Ryan began to read.

On the porch, Mick was looking toward the road. He turned when he heard someone walking out toward him. It was Mary.

He faced her. "Mary, I—"

"No, Mick, I was foolish and selfish. You have a duty, and I had no right to demand anything of you."

He gently took her into his arms.

"You have every right to demand anything of me. After all, you're going to be my wife in a few months. We have a life together to plan."

"It's just... With this war, I just don't—"

He took her chin and lifted it so he could better see her face. "No matter what, I love you, Mary McVinny, and I want you to be my wife."

"I know. I want it too and can't wait for the day we marry."

He hugged her, and they went back into the house.

# CHAPTER EIGHTEEN

On the hot humid day of July 1, a bloody battle began in a little town in Pennsylvania called Gettysburg. That day would host one of the bloodiest battles of the war.

As the reports came in, the family learned that the young Captain Kennedy had been killed in the battle.

Abby was in tears when Ryan broke the news. "He was such a young man. It's so sad, Ryan."

The battle lasted one more day, and as the nation mourned their dead, those left were given the task to heal the wounds.

Abby went to the family graveside behind the house, holding back tears.

"It's just me. I wanted to come up here and talk with you. I know you probably know about the battle. It's such a sad thing. If you should happen to see a young Captain Kennedy up there with you, make him feel welcome, Mama. I guess you also know about Mary and Mick. He really loves her, Papa, and she's so good with Holly. I think he'd be good for Mary also. She's been so alone all this time with Annie gone. Uncle Gideon, I know you're not lonely anymore. You're up there with Mama and Papa and Little Annie. I only wish I'd had more time with you."

She was so busy talking, she didn't hear Ryan walk up behind her. He listened to her as she spoke to those dear souls, who were no longer with them. He felt her pain and wished he could relieve that hurt.

A soft breeze touched her face, and she knew her mother was there. "I know you're here, Mama."

Ryan moved closer. "It's me, Abby."

She turned and saw his face covered in tears. "Ryan, I didn't know you were there."

She felt silly that he had seen her talking to her loved ones.

"You don't need to feel embarrassed," Ryan said. "You have your time with the folks. Take all the time you need."

He went back down to the house. Some time later, Abby returned to the house. Ryan and the children were having supper along with Mick, Mary, and Holly. She slowly made her way through the back door and headed to the dining room.

Mary noticed her first. "I'll get you your plate."

"It's all right. I'm not very hungry."

"Abby, you have to eat."

"I'll be fine. I think I'll go to my room for a while." She continued down the hallway.

Ryan looked at Mick. "I'll go speak with her." He found her sitting on the chair by the window. "Abby, you have to let this go."

"Let it go? I can't help but think of all those men. I think, what if it were you or Ryan. What if Daniel or Thomas have the same fate one day?" She couldn't go on as her sobs turned into tears.

"Abby, it wasn't one of us. We're still here with you." He took her in his arms, holding her close until her sobs settled. "It's all right. I'm here, and I'm not going to leave you ever."

She sighed. "You can't promise that, Ryan."

He looked deep into her eyes, into her very soul. "Abby, I will be with you always. I'll never stop loving you or being here for you."

Some time later, Ryan and Abby went to check on the children already asleep in their rooms. Abby looked at the boys and prayed they would never have to go to war.

Daniel and Thomas were as different as night and day. Even though they were twins, at five years old, they were at the age when they followed Ryan and Uncle Mick wherever they went when they were at home.

She placed a kiss on each forehead and quietly left their room to go into the girls'. Their room was the biggest since all four girls shared it.

After that, they made their way back downstairs into the kitchen. Ryan sat her down as he put the pot on for coffee and proceeded to look for something for Abby to eat. He found the fixings to make a sandwich. He placed the dish in front of Abby, but she didn't seem interested in it.

He sat down beside her. "Abby, I want you to eat."

"I'm just not hungry right now."

"Well, we're gonna sit here until you get hungry."

She looked at him.

"You heard me, Abby. Even if I have to spoon-feed you, you are going to eat."

Just then Mick and Mary walked into the kitchen.

Mick was looking for a snack. "Any of that pie left?" He noticed Abby's plate. "Don't tell me you're not gonna eat that, Abby?"

She looked up at him.

"And don't be giving me one of your looks, 'cause you don't scare me, Abby Lochlan. See, I know what you're really like."

"Really? Do tell me what I'm really like, Mr. Dawson," she said.

He sat down beside her and rested his chin on his elbow. "Well, for one thing, you've been running everything like a man all this time, and it's time you realize you're a lady. You've forgotten what it's like to be a lady. Now, you take your ma, for instance. Molly was a lady with real class. Everyone would think by looking at him that your pa ran the farm. Well, here's the truth: your ma kept it all together and made your pa think he did. It's true, honest. The first day I met her, the way she took control, it was pure genius."

"But Papa always—"

"Your papa always knew it was Molly. That's why, without her, he was lost. He didn't just lose his wife—he lost his world." He gently brushed a strand of her hair from her face. "Come on, Abby, show us how much of Molly is in her girl. Make her proud."

A faint smile appeared on her face, and he looked over at Ryan and smiled himself. "Seems even a lowly jester can make the fair maiden smile." He bent over and gave her a kiss on the cheek.

"Thanks, Mick."

"Anytime, Abby."

The following morning, Abby was in the kitchen, getting breakfast ready.

Mick was the first one to come down for breakfast, looking for some coffee. "Morning, Abby."

Ryan was next to enter, followed by Mary and the kids. Abby looked at the group.

"Well, I think it would be a good idea if Ryan, Mick, and the children go into the dining room and wait for breakfast. Mary and I can handle things in here."

Once they were alone, both girls got started on breakfast. Getting the platter from the cupboard, Mary remembered the day Papa had given it to Mama as a gift. She'd loved that platter and always made sure to have it on the table when it was a special occasion.

"One day, Mama had been in a rush," Mary said. "She grabbed the platter and dropped it, and the plate shattered. She never told Daniel, but next time she went into town, she ordered one from the same catalogue Daniel used. He never knew about the switch."

"Papa never knew?" Abby said.

"Papa never knew about a lot of things. Mama took care of everything but made Papa think he did it all. Papa was a good farmer but not good with the books. It was Mama who made sure all the bills were paid, and paid on time."

"But she always led us all to believe that he did all the dealings for the family."

"He did, but always had Mama read the fine print."

Abby smiled and remembered what Mick had told her the night before. "I like to think that she's here," she said. "Sometimes I think she is, but other times I think it's just a foolish dream."

"Oh, I think sometimes she's here too," Mary said. "I like to think she's watching out for us. I wonder how she'd feel about Mick and me. After all, Mick was married to Jenny."

"He and Jenny were divorced before Mick declared any feeling for you. I think both Mama and Papa would understand."

"I love Holly. She's such a sweet child."

"She is, isn't she? Reminds me a lot of you and Annie when you were her age—so curious and wanting to know everything. I'm waiting for her to ask Papa when she can meet a fella."

They both laughed at that.

# CHAPTER NINETEEN

Sunday service always ended with the congregation praying for the souls of those lost in battle. The list always seemed longer each week. The family sat and listened as Father Cahill called out the names. One hit home.

Lt. Tim McIntire was missing in action. They had no confirmation that he was dead, just missing in action. Young Tim had gone off to join the war and broken Mary's heart. He thought he was going to be a hero.

As always, Father Cahill was at the back of the church as the congregation left after service. Mary had to ask about the McIntire boy.

"Father, I was wondering about that Tim McIntire. Do they know any more than he's missing in action?"

"Mary, I'd like to tell you I know more, but I don't. I only get the list of names each week to post for prayers."

She understood. "Thank you, Father."

They made their way to the general store to pick up a few articles needed at the house. The kids loved candy, and Mick always made sure they got their fill.

Meanwhile, back at the farm, a stranger walked to the back of the house and forced a window open. He reached in and twisted the knob of the back door and let two other men in.

They wore confederate pants and boots and regular shirts. They searched the cupboards and found food. The older one of the group spoke first.

"Good thing you remembered this place, Tim. How did you know these folks?"

Tim McIntire was munching on bread and only stopped to answer the question.

"I was kinda sweet on one of the girls. She was getting serious, and heck, I wanted to enjoy life. The only reason I even gave any attention to her was 'cause her papa left her money."

The other two men smirked and agreed.

"That's the trouble with women. They always want to get serious," the first one said.

"Wait, did you say her papa left her money?" asked the second.

"Yeah, but she wanted to get serious, and I wasn't having any of it. That's why I took off."

The older one looked at him. "So Tim, where are they now?"

"Where are who?"

"The girls. You said there were girls here. Heck, it shouldn't be a total loss coming here."

"The other two are married, Lynch. Mary is the only one single."

"Mary. Now that's a pretty name."

"Trust me, there's nothing pretty about her."

Suddenly the sound of horses alerted the men. They peeked out the window and saw a company of soldiers coming up the road.

Seeing there was no one around, the lieutenant and the sergeant dismounted and knocked on the door.

The sergeant did so three times and called out, "Mrs. Lochlan, is anybody home?"

When there was no answer, the sergeant mounted his horse.

The lieutenant looked at him. "They must be in town. We'll stop back on our way back to the dock. Everything seems to be in order, but I did promise I would notify all citizens about these deserters." He addressed his men. "Company forward."

Tim looked out the window as they rode off. Their getaway using a boat was out of the question. They might have to go back the way they'd come and get to Boston and, from there, hopefully Canada.

The men continued to eat and look for money to help them on their cause.

The afternoon was getting late, and the family had to get back home. With the children all in the back of the wagon, happy with their candy, and Mary and Mick in the second-row seat, Ryan and Abby headed for home. They stopped to say goodbye to Father Cahill one more time.

"Now don't forget, Father," Abby said, "we'd like you to be there next Saturday for supper. It's been a while since you've been out."

"Well Abby, since you put it so nicely, I will be there."

She smiled, and Ryan started the wagon again. Ryan decided to make a short stop at the office just in case something was going on. He and Mick got out and noticed a paper on the board. It was from the lieutenant, telling them to be on the lookout for three deserters that could be in the area. One of them had been identified as Tim McIntire.

Mick looked at Ryan. "We can't let the girls know about this."

"Mick, they have to know if they are in danger—and really in danger since they know the McIntire boy."

"I know. We'll have to think of some way to tell them."

"Well, we'd better get back to the wagon before my wife gets down and sees this notice."

They headed back to the wagon, and Abby asked Ryan, "Is everything all right?"

"Yep, nothing new. I can't wait to get home. I'm starving."

Abby smiled, but she sensed something was not right.

The wagon slowly made its way up the road toward the house.

Tim and the others were on the second floor of the barn, watching them drive up. Lynch looked at the two women.

"They's be some fine-looking women, Tim. And you tell me you didn't want one of them? Why, I'd take either of them."

Tim glared at Lynch. "We came for some grub and money, not the women."

"I hear ya, Tim, but ain't no harm to look, and from where I is sitting, they look good... real good."

"We'll stay in the barn all night and let out before daybreak."

"You suppose the soldier boys are gonna come back this way before we leave?"

"That's why we're leaving before daybreak, Doyle. Wouldn't want to be caught this side of the tracks with a Johnny Reb uniform."

Ryan noticed someone had been in the house when he stepped in the front door. Slowly, he led the children and Mary to the bedroom in the back.

"Abby, keep Mary and the children with you. Mick, get the guns in the cupboard beside the back door."

Mick nodded and got the guns.

Slowly, they made their way through the house—first upstairs, checking the bedrooms, then working down the steps again.

They could see that someone had been in the house, possibly looking for money. Ryan hoped they were gone for the girls' and the children's sake.

They got to the hall when Ryan saw a shadow in the barn. "Mick, in the barn."

They headed outside and were stopped at the steps as two guns were aimed at their skulls.

Tim appeared. "Well, if it isn't Ryan Lochlan and Mick Dawson."

"What do you want, Tim?" Mick asked, barely containing his surprise.

"Funny you should ask that, Mick. You see, my friends and I are in need of a way out of here, and well, with them soldier boys watchin' that dock down there, I figured the only way out is with your help."

"We can't help you get out from the dock. They have patrols there all the time. Your best bet is to backtrack and head to New York and from there, to Canada."

"Do you think I haven't thought of that already?" Tim said. "Enough of this. Let's go back in the house and say hello to the ladies."

They headed back in the house, and Tim opened the bedroom door and let Abby, Mary, and the children out.

"Now, if everyone listens no one will get hurt," Tim said. "We're just all going to spend a little time together until we know it's all right for us to leave here." He winked at Mary. "Hello, Mary. So good to see you. You're looking well."

"What rock did you crawl out from? Last time I saw you, you were spouting how you were going to be a hero. I'm not looking at a hero now."

"You never knew how to keep your mouth shut," Tim spat. "Just like your sister, Abby. I never could figure out what I saw in you, 'cept maybe how much money you have."

She widened her eyes.

"Oh, you didn't know? Well, half the guys who showed any interest in you was 'cause they knew you had come into money. Come on, Mary, did you think anyone wanted you for your beauty? Look at yourself! You're a pitiful creature."

"You are cruel." Mary turned beet red.

"That may be true, Mary, but you were a fool to think I cared for you." He turned to the group. "All right, everyone, let's all move to the front of the house and find a nice, comfortable place on the floor. That means you kids, all in the front."

Abby looked at the children and had them sit in a circle by the fireplace as they did for storytime. Daniel looked at Tim and then back at his mother.

"He's not a nice man, Mama."

"I know, Daniel."

"You named him after your old man," Tim remarked. "That's a nice thing to do. I was named after my old man."

"Oh, I'm sure he's real proud of you."

"Don't know. I shot him when I was fifteen when he came at me with a bullwhip."

"Don't you think you needed it?"

Lynch started to laugh. "I tell you, this little lady's got brass. Tells you right off, Tim."

"Well, this here is the oldest sister. This here is Abby, and she has a lot of the old man in her."

He looked over at Ryan. "Hey Ryan, is it true that she wears the britches in this marriage?"

With all the attention on Abby and Ryan, Mick made a rush for one of the guns, but Lynch hit him on the head with the gun stock. Mick was out cold.

Tim shook his head. "It's a shame. Why do you guys want to be heroes? I told you—once the soldier boys have left, we'll be on our way, and you'll never see us again."

Abby looked at him as Mary tended to Mick. "Can we have that promise in writing?"

"Sass and looks to match," Lynch said. "That's a combination you don't see too often. Sure, we'd like to take you with us. It would sure make those cold nights interesting."

"Lynch, I said we leave the women alone," Tim said.

The sun was setting behind the ridge when they heard the sound of horses coming up the trail. The adults were in the kitchen, having supper with Tim. Tim's friends had guns on the children.

Tim instructed Ryan. "Now, don't forget, one wrong word, and it's bye-bye to these two boys."

The horses came to a stop, and someone knocked on the door.

Abby got up and walked out to answer it. "Can I help you?"

The young lieutenant smiled. "Mrs. Lochlan, I'm sorry to bother you, but we have to alert all families in the area about the deserters that are somewhere around. One of them is Tim McIntire, who was thought to be missing in action."

"Oh really, we heard his name at service today. And you say he could be around here?"

"Well, we were told to notify everyone, ma'am."

"I see. Well, thank you for letting us know, Lieutenant." She closed the door and walked back into the dining room.

"You did real good, Mrs. Lochlan. Real good."

Halfway down the road but out of sight from the house, the sergeant stopped his horse. He'd felt something brushing past his cheeks, and he could've sworn he heard a woman's voice.

"What is it, Sergeant?" The lieutenant stopped too.

The sergeant realized something. "Didn't you find the scene back there a bit strange? I have been to Mrs. Lochlan's home on many occasions, and there was never a time she didn't offer something to us. She gave us breakfast one morning."

"And your point now, Sergeant?"

"Something is wrong there, Lieutenant. Could be they're in trouble. It's worth a look."

"All right, Sergeant. Take a few men and head back. If you need reinforcements, have one come back. We'll be here waiting."

"Jones, Harper, Roberts, Lucas, come back with me."

They returned to the house, coming via the back road. As they reached the turnoff, they dismounted and walked the rest of the way.

# CHAPTER TWENTY

Back inside the house, the deserters were enjoying their meal and not looking out the window.

"Eat up boys," Tim said to the other two. "Don't know when we'll have a fine meal like this again."

"That's true," Lynch said, "unless we's to take one of these ladies—"

Tim stopped him. "I said we leave the women alone, Lynch. Don't let me tell you another time."

"Sure, sure, I understand, Tim. No ladies."

Somehow, Lynch didn't sound as though he'd keep his promise.

The sergeant and his men were moving closer to the house. He saw the men at the table, but he also saw the children there. The sergeant wouldn't dare risk the children in the line of fire. The only thing he could do was to wait and figure out their next move. Inside the house, Abby and Mary sat with the children on the far side of the room.

"What turned you into this, Tim?" Mary asked.

"The war!" Tim answered. "There was no adventure, no honor, no glory. All there was was death everywhere. You turned, and you were faced with it—young men dying all around you, and you wondered, would you be next?"

"I can see where that would take the adventure out of it, but what were you thinking when you signed up? Not to mention, you signed up in the Confederacy."

"Well, I heard that this was only gonna be for a few weeks, and we'd all be coming home as heroes."

Abby started to feel sorry for the young man. Tim had seen this as a chance to be someone, and it backfired.

"So you did this for no reason other than—"

"You got it, Mrs. Lochlan. I did it to become a hero. There ain't many of us who were left with money like you and your sisters were. I thought I'd come back a hero and maybe even start to court your sister, and maybe even marry her. Lord knows no one else seemed interested. She's not like you or Jenny. She's rather plain, and well, a man likes a wife that has some looks or, in this case, money." He looked at Mary then back at Abby. "Sorry to hurt anyone's feelings, but I'm only saying what I see."

Lynch realized saw how dark it was getting outside; soon it would be dark enough for them to leave.

"Hey Tim, we'd better think about how we will leave here."

"I'm surprised at you, Lynch. Why, these good people are gonna offer us their horses. Am I right, Mrs. Lochlan?"

"Of course, Mr. McIntire."

She glanced out the window and saw a shadow looking back at Tim. She wanted to let Ryan know what was going on but had to do it without letting Tim know. She picked up one of Molly's favorite books, *Looking through the Window*, and handed it to Ryan.

"Ryan, why don't you read the children a story?"

Ryan took the book and saw Abby nod.

"You don't mind my husband reading to the children, do you, Tim?"

"No, not at all, Mrs. Lochlan. We should be leaving in a while, and then you and your family can go back to leading normal lives. By the way, thank you for the three horses out there in the corral."

"You're welcome."

The sergeant slowly moved back and motioned for his men to do the same.

"Doyle, go out there and get those horses saddled."

Doyle nodded and left through the back door, leaving only Tim and Lynch inside the house.

Tim looked at Abby and smiled. "Well, Mrs. Lochlan, looks like we'll be leaving your company, and it's been a pleasant evening. One more thing: I would appreciate if all of you would stay in the house as we leave. It would be a bad move on your part if you didn't."

The sergeant and his men had moved down the road, far enough to keep the family safe.

Tim made his way to the front door. "Thank you again, Mrs, Lochlan."

With that, he was out the door, and they started to ride down the road. Mick was about to get up and follow them when Mary pulled him down on the chair.

"No, Mick!" she said.

Abby filled him in. "There are soldiers outside who are waiting to capture them as soon as they leave the house. I saw the shadows from the window."

Suddenly, they heard the sounds of gunfire and then silence. Abby said a prayer for Tim. She felt a sadness for the boy, who'd wanted so much to be someone and never really could.

The sound of horses came from up the road, and then the familiar voice of the sergeant called out to them. "Mrs. Lochlan, are all of you alright?"

Abby, Ryan, Mick and Mary came out the door.

"Hello, Sergeant," Abby said. "I'm so glad to see you came back."

"Yes, ma'am. I told the lieutenant that it wasn't like you to not offer us some refreshment. You always are very hospitable to us."

"Thank the Lord you got the clue. You have to understand, we had the children in there also."

"I understand, ma'am, and we took that into consideration when we saw what was going on inside."

"Please, on your way back, all of you stop in for refreshments."

Mary came out with a basket of food for the sergeant.

"Sergeant, please take this as our thanks for your help. Tim McIntire, he…"

"He's fine, ma'am, but will be spending some time in prison for what he did."

Both Abby and Mary said a silent prayer that he would be spared death.

# CHAPTER TWENTY ONE

The war had ended, and the nation had the arduous task of putting itself back together again. Mick was given orders to report to Washington for a possible assignment in the capital.

Mick and Mary married quickly. Before long, they were on the boat to New York and then to Washington by way of railroad.

Abby was saddened by her sister's move, but she knew it had to be. Both sisters promised to keep in touch, and of course Holly was always welcome when school had a break.

Mary hugged Abby one more time. "I already miss you."

"I do too, but we will keep in touch, and Mick says we'll be down here at least once a month."

"Take care of yourself, Mary."

She walked over to Mick, who was talking to Ryan, and she hugged him. "Mick, you take good care of my baby sister, or I'll come to Washington and take her home."

"Abby, trust me, I love her as much as Sir Lancelot over there loves you. I can't thank you for all you've done for me, for Holly. You did your mama proud, and I can see why Ryan loves you. Oh yeah, I'm gonna let you in on a little secret: I do too."

He gave her a kiss on the cheek then boarded the boat with Mary and Holly.

On the ride back home, many memories came to Abby's mind: the three young girls they used to be, sitting at the supper table every night, listening to their papa. Always at the other end of the table was Mama, always calm and in control. Her smile would light up a room, her soft voice welcoming all who came to the door.

She thought of Jenny and how she'd found her life with the rich better than one with her family. She thought also of Ryan, a young man who'd come from Ireland looking for a new life and who'd walked into hers and never gave her a moment of regret.

Days turned to weeks that turned into months.

Mick and Mary were happy in Washington, and their family was growing. They welcomed Maryanne and newborn Peyton Michael into the family.

Holly was fourteen. The three McVinny girls had grown up as well. Abby and Mary had started their own families and carried on what Molly and Daniel had started.

Sitting on the porch, admiring Molly's roses, Abby was teaching her girls the art of knitting.

Molly looked at her mother. "Mama, did you really have to learn this?"

"Yes I did, and I had to learn how to sew and crochet. These are skills that young ladies learn."

"Well, I don't want to be a lady, then."

Abby laughed and remembered how it had taken her a whole three weeks just to learn how to knit and purl.

Annie looked up in frustration. She had lost a knit, which threw her whole pattern off again. "Mama, there has to be an easier way."

"I'm afraid not, Annie. This is the only way it's done."

Annie looked at her needles again. "It will take forever to knit a sweater, and it won't be ready this winter."

Abby smiled. She knew how frustrating it could be to learn the knit-purl stitch. "Girls, I think we should take a break on this for today and check on those pies. They should be cool by now."

Ryan had taught the boys all he knew about farming, and Daniel had a real love for the land. Thomas, on the other hand, seemed to like the animals. Both were an enormous help to Ryan on the farm. Finally, after all those years, the farm was starting to pay off and show a profit.

Twice a month, Ryan and Daniel would take some of their vegetables to the dock, where they were sent to New York to a market. One day, as Ryan was standing by the wagon, he noticed a woman coming off the ship.

She looked like Jenny. He looked again. It was Jenny. Dark hair, blue eyes that seemed to have faded, a complexion painted with makeup. She saw him and waved and called out to him.

"Ryan, Ryan!" She walked up to him and gave him a hug. "Oh Ryan, it's so good to see you. My, you look wonderful."

"It's good to see you too, Jenny. Well, what brings you here?"

She smiled at him. "Oh Ryan, always the joker. I came to see my daughter. Tell me, how does she look? Oh, I bet she's a beauty."

"Well, Jenny, we haven't seen Holly in two years."

"What do you mean?" Jenny furrowed the brows on her still-beautiful face.

"Holly lives in Washington with Mick and Mary and their children."

The look on her face was more pain than shock. "Mary? My baby sister is married to my husband?"

"Ex-husband, Jenny."

She started to walk away and then turned back. "Take me to the hotel. I need to make arrangements to be on the next ship to New York, then the train to Washington."

"Jenny, why are you doing this?" Ryan asked.

She gave him a sharp look. "Your wife had this all planned, and I will deal with her after I get my daughter back with me in London."

"You can find your own way to the hotel," Ryan said. "I won't help you hurt Holly."

"How dare you talk to me like that?"

"You're my wife's sister, and I have to show you some respect 'cause of Abby. But don't you be talking down to me like that. You left your husband and little girl. Maybe you had a good reason, but it seems to me you're a bit too late now. Mary's done a fine job raising Holly, as fine a job as if she was her own girl. Mick has found love in Mary, the kind of love he thought he found with you. Let me ask you—and the truth this time—why did you come back?"

A vicious look came across her face. "I came for the money. I'm broke."

"Mick gave his share of your pa's money to Holly. Since Mary has a share from your father, Mick and her decided to put their shares in a trust for the children."

"Well, fine, I'll take Holly with me and be in charge of her money."

"Holly doesn't get her money until she's twenty-one, and Mick and Mary made the judge the guardian over the inheritance." He climbed onto the wagon and picked up Daniel, who was on his way up to meet him. "Come on, Daniel, we'd better get home before the storm hits."

"What storm, Pa? There's not a cloud in the sky."

When Ryan got home, he told Abby the whole incident. Abby knew Jenny could be heartless, but coming back just for the money was too much, even for her. She'd squandered all her money, and she wanted her daughter's inheritance.

"You have to send a wire to Mick and warn him."

"I will in the morning."

Jenny did get on the train to Washington to confront Mary and Mick but never got there. Somewhere outside of Philadelphia, the train derailed, and there were no survivors.

Jenny McVinny Dawson stepped onto that train and into the eternity met by her mother and father.

And so the McVinny girls once again gathered to lay one of them to rest. That time, Abby said the psalm. Mick, Mary, and the children were there. Fourteen-year-old Holly grieved for the woman she'd never really known. Mick grieved for the wife he'd lost long before that day, and Mary grieved for the sister who'd helped raise her after their mother passed. If Jenny had come, as they'd expected her to, Mary would've said her piece and told her to scram. But now that Jenny was dead, Mary could only remember the good old times, back when

Jenny was a sweet older sister to her. She cried deeply, holding onto Mick.

Abby's loss was for the sister she'd once known, not the cold woman she had become. She prayed that Jenny would be forgiven for her sins and that she was up there in the arms of their mother. Their mother had told them that when a person died, their loved ones would be waiting for them on the other side, to help them cross over. Abby closed her eyes for a moment and thought what a great moment it would be to be reunited with the family.

Unlike other times, that service was small and simple. Mick, Mary, and the children were back on the train that afternoon. At the train station, the sisters hugged each other one more time before Mary boarded the train.

"We'll see each other soon, Abby. I promise."

Mick shook hands with Ryan. "Thanks for all your help on this, Ryan. I didn't know what to think when the railroad people came to my house. I certainly didn't expect it."

As Abby boarded the train, they found their seats, looked out the windows, and waved. Abby's girls had missed Holly so. After all, they'd all shared the same room for years.

That night, sitting outside on the porch, Ryan had his arms around Abby as he usually did. She looked up at the night sky. She had always loved the inky black sky with hundreds of tiny lights against it.

A shooting star passed by, and Abby said a prayer. That was what her mother had said to do when she saw a shooting star. But Abby felt the star was Jenny telling her she was up there with Mama, Papa and Annie.

She had no idea what the next day would be like, but she did know Ryan would be there beside her just as he was at that moment. She nestled in his arms and felt his heartbeat, slow and steady, always there for her.

He looked down at her. "Comfortable?"

"Yes, thank you."

"You know, Abby, I've been thinking. We never really had a honeymoon, and now that the kids are getting older, maybe we can take a short trip to New York for a day. The ship comes right here to the dock. I mean, it's only an idea."

She looked at him in surprise. "Ryan, in all these sixteen years I have never wanted to be anywhere but on this farm and with you. For you to ask me this is so sweet. I never really thought about a honeymoon. Every day with you is a honeymoon, and I don't need anything special, just to know you're here and we are happy and the children are healthy."

He looked at her and smiled. "I truly believe you're right when you said I have the luck of the Irish. It was that luck that brought me to you."

"Oh, really? I thought it was wanting to use my papa's road."

"The road was an excuse. I really wanted to see you." Ryan thought about Daniel and Molly and how they had welcomed him into the family so warmly all those years before. "I still feel they're here with us, your folks and mine. I wish you had met them. They would have loved you. I was an only child, and to have you give them grandchildren, they would have been so happy."

Ryan rarely spoke about his parents. She wondered if he was feeling sorry that he had lost them so young.

The past was the past, and neither Abby nor Ryan could do anything. What they could anticipate was the future. She closed her eyes and imagined what awaited them. With the children growing, one day they would leave, yet she and Ryan would still be here together looking at the night sky.

As the years passed by, Abby and Ryan still remained on the farm. It seemed like only yesterday when three little girls tried to get their daddy to smile. Today, one of them was going to try to make sure her daddy didn't cry.

The first of the Lochlan girls to be married was Meghan. On that cold winter's day, all eyes were on Ryan as he escorted his Meghan down the aisle to become the wife of Adam Bradford, a young congressman from Pennsylvania. They'd met the previous summer at a party hosted by her aunt and uncle, the Dawsons. The young congressman found her enchanting and came to Fall River to ask her parents for her hand in marriage. The announcement was done tastefully since they kept the ceremony a private affair.

Meghan Christine Lochlan, the daughter of Mr. and Mrs. Ryan Lochlan of Fall River, Massachusetts, was married to Congressman Adam Bradford, the junior congressman from Pennsylvania, on November 12 at his parents' home. The young couple exchanged their vows in front of family and friends, and a small reception followed. The groom's parents planned on giving them a dinner the next week. The couple would be dividing their time between Pennsylvania and Washington during the year.

It saddened Abby to think of her daughter being so far away, but Adam promised they would be back in Massachusetts at least for the family holidays.

The next of the girls to leave was Molly, two years later. Molly had met Braxton Calhan in New York at a lecture. The young man had fallen in love with her on the spot and proposed to her on the stairs of the hotel. It took eighteen months before Molly said yes.

Little did she know at the time that Braxton was the son of Carter Braxton Calhan—of the law firm of Calhan, Stamford, Willis, and Finer, one of New York's prestigious law firms.

Braxton was a junior partner in the firm and was set to open the firm's branch in Boston. Carter Calhan found Molly not only beautiful but an important asset to the business, who would do well among Boston's elite. She fit the role well: born in Massachusetts, her family had been there for years, and her father had worked for the railroad. She was tailor-made for the role.

On the day of the wedding, the entire backyard was made completely into an outdoor garden with roses, yellow roses, everywhere. Meghan and Annie were upstairs with Molly, helping her get ready. Meghan, the matron of honor, dressed in a lovely shade of gold, and Annie had a bronze-colored dress, as did Cousin Holly, who had come to join the girls on the special day. Abby had a lovely shade of green lace on her gown. The Calhans had the food delivered from New York by boat, which docked at the harbor at Fall River. Guests came by ship, and horse-drawn carriages brought them to the main house. It truly looked like a royal wedding. Even the various tabloids covered the event. The notice read:

"Molly Lochlan, daughter of Abigail and Ryan Lochlan of Fall River, Massachusetts, was united in marriage today to Braxton Wilson Calhan, the son of Carter Braxton Calhan and Susanne Wilson Calhan of New York.

"The bride is the granddaughter of Daniel and Molly McVinny of Virginia and the daughter of Abigail and Ryan Lochlan of Fall River. Miss Lochlan is the niece of Mr. Michael Dawson of the State Department and the sister-in-law of Congressman Adam Bradford.

"The ceremony was held at the bride's family home, officiated by Father Edward Cahill. The couple plan to reside in Boston, where the groom will open a branch of the firm of Calhan, Stamford, Willis, and Finer and run our branch office for the firm."

The day seemed as if it would never stop. The food, the music, the people... the wedding was more than Abby could have ever imagined.

When the guests had left, and no one was left to entertain, Abby sat on a chair under a trellis of yellow roses. Ryan smiled at her. There was no question she looked beautiful.

He walked up to her and offered her his hand. "A dance, my lady?"

Although she was tired, she got up, and he pulled her close to him. Without music, they slowly swayed to the music they heard in their heads.

Abby placed her head on his chest and closed her eyes. "Ryan, have I told you what I love about you?"

He tilted his head at her. "My charm and good looks?"

"Come on, I'm serious."

He stopped dancing and looked deep into her eyes, and what beautiful eyes they were. "Tell me, my sweet Abby, what do you love about me?"

"I love you because you always made me feel safe and special. A lady."

"You are my lady, Abby. My fair lady. I would lay down my life for you, and I wish I could have spared you the sorrow of losing your mama and Annie so young. I wish I could make all your dreams come true and prevent any tears to your eyes."

She put her arms around his waist and held on to him tight. "I love you, Ryan. Don't ever doubt that."

"I never will, my sweet Abby."

As they started to walk back into the house, Annie was going up the stairs when she saw her parents. "Night, Mama and Papa." She stopped and kissed each one on the cheek then continued up the stairs.

"I wonder when will we see our Annie get married?" Abby wondered.

"We just had two of them leave us," Ryan said. "Let's not get too anxious to lose the last one."

"I know, but I would like to see her settled and married. She's my little Annie."

# Chapter Twenty Two

Two years later, Ryan and Abby were blessed with their first grandson, from their son Daniel and his lovely wife Jeanne.

The boy was named Peter Ryan Lochlan, after both grandfathers, and the Lochlan name would carry on. The entire town of Fall River was invited to the baptism and celebration at the main house. Carriages were lined up and down the street and up the drive for the event.

All the Lochlan children, including Thomas, was there. Thomas, who had been out west learning about cattle ranching, dropped everything to come home for the event.

He was sitting in the family dining room, talking to his parents and Annie. "When I got the wire from Daniel, I knew I had to be here. I mean, how often does the Lochlan family have another boy? Besides, it's time I came home and had some of Mama's good cooking. Not to mention, I miss all of you. Yes, even you, Annie."

Mary and Mick had their share of excitement also. Holly had announced her engagement to Jason Holmes, a young man who worked at the state department with Mick. Mary wanted Holly to be married at the family home in Fall River, and Abby was thrilled.

Annie got together with her sisters to give Holly a shower, and Maryanne was asked to be a junior bridesmaid, which thrilled the girl.

Everything was going smoothly when Molly got out of the carriage, walked up the steps, and fainted.

Abby called for her husband. "Ryan! It's Molly."

From the back of the house, Ryan and Daniel came running out.

"What happened?" Ryan asked.

"She was just getting out of the wagon, and then she fainted."

Ryan looked at Daniel. "Go into town, get the doc, and find Braxton. He should be coming by ship at the dock."

Ryan picked her up and carried her into the house. She regained consciousness when everyone was hovering over her. "What? Did I miss something?" Molly said.

Brax was looking at her with concern. "You got off the carriage and fainted," he said.

"Oh, that," Molly said. "Nothing to worry about. I've done it before. Seems when I get up too fast, I faint. It's got something to do with being pregnant."

"You're pregnant?" Braxton exclaimed. "And you didn't tell me?"

"Really, Brax, it's no earth-shattering revelation. Women all over the world get pregnant."

"Maybe so, but I'm not married to all of them. I'm married to only you."

Ryan looked at Abby and smiled. "She's definitely your daughter."

With Molly confined to bed by Braxton, Annie and Abby's job was to get the rooms ready for the family's arrival.

Mick and Mary arrived by train later that afternoon. The big room was for Mick, Mary, Peyton, and Maryanne since it was the biggest bedroom and could fit all four. Mick's old room was going to Meghan and Adam. Annie's old room was upstairs, and Molly and Braxton had the twins' old room.

That night after everyone had gone to bed, Mary and Abby sat by the fire.

"Oh Abby, it seems like only yesterday we were sitting here talking about how to tell Papa we wanted to go to the social. I can even see him telling us it was not a place for us because we were too young."

"I can remember the look on Papa's face when Ryan walked into the dining room that morning. He was madder than a wet hen, and there was nothing he could do with Mama there."

"You know," Mary said. "I think I knew you loved him when Annie said she thought he was pretty. The look on your face said that she was absolutely right."

"I don't know how he could have thought anything about me since, when I first met him, I couldn't say a word. I was totally in shock. I felt he thought I was some freak."

"Oh, I don't think he thought that of you. Mick told me that they would tease him and call him Lancelot, who would fight the dragons for his fair maiden."

"That poor man... what he went through." Abby smiled wistfully.

# CHAPTER TWENTY THREE

The morning of Holly's wedding started with a perfect sunrise. Abby and Mary were up at dawn, preparing not only breakfast but the food for the reception and, of course, the cake. Mary and Abby had just finished decorating it. Mary was good at making roses out of icing. She placed the bride and groom figurines on top of the cake, and they'd both stood back to admire it when Ryan and Mick walked in.

Ryan ran his finger up the side of the bottom layer and licked the frosting from it.

Abby yelled at him. "Ryan!"

"What?"

"What are you doing? That's Holly's wedding cake."

"It's only a little bit. You can fix it. By the way, it tastes great."

She slapped his hand away when he went in for another taste. "Both of you, out of this kitchen, and don't go near this cake again."

"But Abby, we came for some breakfast."

"In the dining room. Not in here." She noticed him looking at the ham, already sliced. "Don't even think it, Lochlan. Mick, you keep on moving too."

Ryan protested, "Honest, Abby, I just came in for a—"

She gently pushed them toward the door. "Yes, yes, coffee is in the dining room. Annie can get you anything else."

As they left, both Abby and Mary shook their heads. They wondered at times which ones were really the children. A memory of Molly, their mother, catching the girls licking a spoon of cake batter put a smile on Mary's face.

Abby looked at her. "Mama?"

Mary nodded as she wiped a tear from her eye. "I always feel like she's close."

Abby nodded. "I know. There are times I even hear her voice."

Mary looked at her. "Oh, thank God, Abby. Thank God. I swear when it first happened to me, I thought I was losing my mind. It was my wedding day—it was almost a whisper, but I heard Mama say she was happy and I was doing the right thing marrying Mick."

"I heard her on my wedding day too and then again when I found out I was having the twins. It's like she's here, watching over us."

They looked down at the cake when Annie came in and said, "Mama, there are some guests arriving."

"Guests?"

They followed Annie to Father Cahill and a young man.

"Ah, Abby and Mary, I hope you don't mind," Father Cahill said, "but I took the liberty of taking my nephew Jack along. He is here on a visit from Cambridge. He's a graduate from Harvard."

Abby smiled at the young man. "Welcome, Jack. This is my sister, Mary, mother of the bride, and my daughter Annie, who will be happy to help you with anything you need."

"Thank you," Jack said graciously.

Father Cahill and Jack followed Annie as Mary and Abby moved closer to the stairs.

"A nice-looking boy, and single," Mary whispered.

"Really?" Abby said innocently. "I didn't notice."

Mary looked at Abby. "You must be slipping, Abby not noticing a good-looking man—that'll be the day."

Abby placed her hands on Mary's shoulders and smiled.

"It's been a long time since I looked at men. Come on, baby sister, let's say hello and then get ready for Holly's big day."

They went to mingle with the guests. Mary and Abby were busy greeting a few close friends from town when she saw Ryan talking with Father Cahill and his nephew. Ryan motioned for her to come over.

"I see you've met Father Cahill's nephew," Abby said.

"Yes, did you know he's been offered the position of history professor at Harvard next semester?"

Abby smiled at the young man again. She had to admit that Mary was right. He was quite good looking: tall, fair haired, light eyes—not blue, more of a gray shade.

"No, I didn't," she replied, looking at Jack. "That's wonderful. Tell me, what era of history do you most enjoy?"

"I enjoy European history, Mrs. Lochlan. I find it extremely fascinating."

"Yes, I can understand that, and please call me Abby. Everyone does."

His expression relaxed as he smiled back.

"My full name is Jackson," he said. "My mother was related to Andrew Jackson, but I just use Jack."

"Well, Jack, I was just going to tell you make yourself at home. If you need anything, just ask Annie. She'll be here for a bit longer, then she's got to run and get ready for the wedding. Ryan can help if you need anything, too. If you'll excuse me, I've got to get the mother of the bride together."

"Thanks so much."

She headed up the stairs and took a quick peek into the girls' room before going into Mary's. She walked in and found Mary just sitting there, looking into the mirror. Curious, she walked up to her. "Mary? Mary!"

Mary looked up at her with dazed eyes.

"Abby, I hear her. She was here."

"Mary, calm down. Of course she's here. It's a wedding day. You know she wouldn't miss a wedding, especially a granddaughter."

"It was still a bit unsettling when I heard it."

Abby hugged her. "I know, but it's all right, Mary. She loves you. Now, let's get you dressed. We have a wedding to attend."

Abby walked to the closet and brought out Mary's gown. Mary had had all the dresses made in Washington. The bridal party was all in light blue as it was Holly's favorite color. Mary's gown was in sapphire-blue satin, with a velvet jacket to go with it. Abby's gown was in midnight blue. Holly had remembered how her aunt loved the midnight sky, and her neckline and sleeves had hundreds of tiny glass beads that looked like stars glowing.

Abby brightened at the sight of Mary dressed in her gown.

"You look radiant!"

Mary looked at herself in the mirror. "You don't think it's a bit too much?"

"Not at all."

Abby got her dress and proceeded to put it on. She walked past Mary, who was fixing her hair, and stopped to look in the mirror.

"Abby," Mary exclaimed. "I can't believe it. You look just like Mama!"

For the first time, Abby really examined her reflection. In a brief instant, an image, although almost transparent, appeared beside Abby's reflection. Wide eyed, both girls looked at the image then at each other.

"Abby, do you see it?"

"Yes. It's okay, Mary."

"Are you sure? I mean, I've never seen anything like that before."

"It's all right. After all, it's not real, and it's Mama. She would never hurt us."

In a blink of an eye, the image was gone. Both girls took a deep breath, and decided not to talk about it.

They walked across the hall to check on the girls. When they opened the door, Holly was standing by a full mirror, looking beautiful. She turned to her mother and aunt in awe.

"You two look beautiful, even better than me, and I'm the bride."

Abby smiled. "Oh, I wouldn't say that. Well, we're going to head down and out back when the music starts. It's time for you girls to start."

"Yes, Mama. I think we've got it, but you make sure you and Aunt Mary don't cry through the whole ceremony."

"Oh, don't be so fresh. And you know your Aunt Mary is gonna cry. We'll see you downstairs. Don't forget, Holly, smile." Mary and Abby headed down the stairs and were escorted to their seats by Daniel and young Peyton Dawson.

Someone knocked on the door. Holly turned and saw Mick peeking in.

"Are we about ready, princess?"

"Yes, Pa."

"You look so beautiful, Holly. You grew up to be a fine young lady and have made me proud."

"Thanks, Pa."

"Come on. Let's go show them, my pretty lady."

He offered his arm to her, and they walked out the door.

# CHAPTER TWENTY FOUR

Mary was sitting in the front row of chairs along with Ryan, Abby, and Thomas. Slowly, the procession of girls appeared at the doorway, starting with little Maryanne. The groomsmen waited at the foot of the stairs and walked up the aisle with their partners until the only pair left was Holly and her father.

The music began, and Mick and Holly walked up the aisle. Abby beamed at Mary, thinking how she'd done a fine job raising Holly; she was truly her mother.

After the ceremony, Ryan was still looking at that cake when it was brought out and placed on the table. Abby swore she would tie his hands if he went near it while the wedding photos were being taken.

After the first dance of the bride and groom, the bride took her father onto the dance floor, and the groom took his mother.

Ryan saw everyone was on the dance floor and looked over at Abby. "Shall we join them, me lady?"

"I'd love to, Ryan."

He offered her his hand and led her out onto the floor. He held her close, and they moved to the music. He looked into her eyes, smiling as if he still couldn't believe his luck after all those years.

"I know I've said it so many times, but Abigail Peyton McVinny Lochlan, I love you, and you look beautiful today. That dress is really you. It looks like you took all the stars in the sky and had them surround you."

"I love it when you talk like that. You're such a romantic. And thank you. The dress credit goes to Holly. She picked it because she knew I liked the night sky and the stars."

"Well, don't tell anyone, but you outshine any star."

Mick tapped Ryan's shoulder. "If you don't mind, I'd like to dance with your fair maiden."

"Only if you promise not to ride off with her."

"Me? I'll have you know I'm Sir Galahad, a noble knight of the round table. Besides, I have my own fair maiden."

"Will one of you leave so we don't look silly on this dance floor?" Abby said.

"All right, my lady," said Ryan. "I will leave you, but I shall return soon, to claim you as my true love."

Mick took Abby's hand and danced with her. "I wanted to thank you for everything, for helping when Jenny left, taking care of Holly like she was your own, and Mary's and my wedding. You are quite a lady, Abby."

"It was a pleasure to do all of it for all of you. We're family, and we help each other, no matter what."

The reception slowly wound down, and the guests were saying their goodbyes. It was time for the newlyweds to leave, as well.

As the couple bade farewell to the family, tears came to Mary's eyes.

Abby squeezed her hand. "Hang on, Mary. Wait until she leaves."

Thomas drove the carriage up to the front steps. The girls were ready with the rice and were waiting eagerly for them to come out.

Holly hugged her Aunt Abby. "I can never thank you for all you did for me when I was growing up. I love you and Uncle Ryan."

"Honey, we love you and are so happy for you and want you to be happy."

"I am." She hugged Ryan and kissed his cheek. "Thank you, Uncle Ryan."

He helped her into the carriage, and they were on their way. Ryan and Abby watched the carriage fade down the road and out of sight. They made their way back to the house.

"Can I interest you in a walk?" Ryan asked Abby. "It looks like a nice night, and look at all the stars out here. Maybe not as many as on your dress, but they're out there."

"I'd like that."

They made their way around the house. "The sky was indeed beautiful tonight. Almost as beautiful as you. But then again, nothing will be as beautiful as you."

"Oh Ryan Lochlan, how you do go on."

He stopped, lowered his head, and kissed her. After all those years, he still felt the same as he did the first day he saw her. She looked into his eyes and knew she would love him all her days and never tire of him.

Annie came out onto the porch and saw her parents in one of their moments.

"I hope I'm not interrupting something, but we're all having cake and coffee in the dining room if you care to join us."

"That sounds like a good idea. We'll be right in."

When Ryan and Abby came in, Mary gave them both a smile with a knowing look. "Been looking at the stars again, Abby? It is a nice night for it."

Annie passed pieces of cake to her mother and her father as Ryan sat down.

"Well, it was a lovely wedding, and I just want to go on the record saying that you ladies looked absolutely lovely. Don't you agree, Mick?"

"I certainly do, Ryan. We are married to two lovely women."

# CHAPTER TWENTY FIVE

Molly gave birth to a beautiful baby girl on a cold and snowy day. Of course, Abby and Ryan couldn't make it up to Boston due to the weather, but the wire Braxton sent informed them that both the mother and child were fine. No name had been chosen yet, but Molly would let them know when they did.

As Abby sat by the fire, Ryan looked out the window. "I promise you, Abby, we'll get up there as soon as the weather lets up."

True to his promise, he got Abby to Boston to see her granddaughter within four days after the snow started melting. When Abby walked into the house, the baby stopped crying, and there was silence.

Sara Elizabeth was content to have her grandmother hold her, and Abby was convinced that she'd stopped the crying, and no one could tell her different. Of course, Molly knew the problem was colic but was willing to let Abby have her moment. Abby gave her the nickname Sassy, and Sassy she became.

Abby found it hard to say goodbye after only four days, but Molly promised they would see her and the other family members for Easter. The following month, *The Boston Herald* ran the announcement of Sara's birth:

"Mr. and Mrs. Braxton Calhan's first child was the granddaughter of Carter Braxton Calhan and Susanne Wilson Calhan of New York and Ryan and Abigail Lochlan of Fall River, Massachusetts."

Once back at home, Abby noticed how quiet the house seemed with everyone gone. Annie had gone to Washington to visit her Aunt Mary, where she got to visit with Holly and Jack.

Thomas had gone with Annie and was contemplating going to a military academy. Uncle Mick thought it was a good idea on Thomas's part, and through his connections, Mick was able to get him into West Point for the next semester. That alone would have made his grandparents proud. Abby felt they would have been proud of all their grandchildren.

But that living room, which had always been bustling with laughter and music, was as quiet as a morgue. All that was left were memories tucked into the walls of each room.

Above the mantel were pictures of the family, including Molly and Daniel, their girls, and their grandchildren. Abby looked at the wedding picture of her father and mother. Her father had truly been a handsome man, and her mother was radiant. They were such a handsome couple.

Abby's favorite photo was of her and her sisters all sitting on the sofa. They looked like angels. The photographer had captured Annie's smile perfectly, and she looked as if she was smiling back at Abby—as if the image had a life of its own.

Abby looked at her own wedding photo for a long time. She felt as if she was looking at someone else. Thirty years before, she had said "I do" to that man, who had come to her house to ask her father's permission to let the railroad use their road. Remembering the story of how they met never ceased to warm her heart.

Ryan came up to her as she was still looking at the photos. "There's a handsome-looking couple."

"Do you think so, after all these years?"

"I still think the lady in that photograph is still as beautiful as the day I married her."

She turned around and put her arms around him. "You always know what to say, Mr. Lochlan."

For the past year, Annie had been seeing Professor Jack Cahill.

He had seen Annie when she had gone to Boston to see her sister, but again time was not on his side. Finally, Jack decided to take some time off and visit his uncle down in Fall River. He rode up to the Lochlan home that spring morning and saw Abby pruning the flowers in the flower garden.

He rode up to the porch and greeted Abby. "Morning, Mrs. Lochlan."

"Why, hello, Jack. How have you been? I haven't seen you since Holly's wedding."

"Yes, it's been a while. I came over, hoping to see if Miss Annie were here."

"I'm sorry, Jack, she's in town and had to get a few things. She should be back soon. If you like, you can wait."

"No, I'll just go back to town. I'll run into her one day. Do tell her I stopped by, Mrs Lochlan. Have a nice day."

"You too, Jack."

He rode off as Ryan came out to the porch.

"You have a young gentleman caller, my lady?"

"Not me, but I think our little Annie does."

"Our Annie?"

She put down the pruning shears and sat on the chair. "Ryan, at times I wonder if you even listen to what I say."

"I always listen to what you say. I just don't always answer."

She gave him a look.

"Aw, come on, Abby, you know I'm only funnin' with ya. Matter of fact, I think we should have a party and invite everyone, even that young man that was just here. Maybe we can get him and Annie in the same town or maybe even the same house for a change."

"What do you think of him?" Abby asked.

"He seems alright. A bit sheepish, but if Annie likes him..."

"That's just it. I'm not sure she even cares about him."

An hour passed, and Annie still hadn't gotten back from town. Abby was starting to worry. She thought Ryan had better go check on her.

"I would feel better if you would take a ride toward town and see if you see her coming."

"I'll go, but you know she's fine. Probably stopped for some critter."

He found Tom, and they headed out in search of Annie. They knew she would be on the main road since she was using the wagon.

"She's probably still in town," Tom said. "You know how she gets to talking and forgets about the time."

"That's what I told your ma, but you know how she is. She's always been a bit protective with Annie."

"I tell you one thing. Annie's gonna be mad at us when we catch up to her 'cause Mama sent us out to fetch her."

"You got that one right."

They got almost halfway to town and still found no sign of Annie or the wagon. Around the final bend was when they saw it—the wagon had overturned, and Annie was underneath.

# CHAPTER TWENTY SIX

Ryan was the first to get to her. Tom rushed over, bringing his canteen of water with him.

"Annie," Ryan called out. "Annie!"

Her eyes were closed, and she appeared to be unconscious. He tried to lift the wagon, but it was too heavy. He also saw a large crate resting on her left leg. It was pinning her under the wagon. "Tim, I need you to see if you can lift this wagon just enough to get her out from under it."

"Will do."

He remounted his horse and lassoed the wheel of the wagon. Slowly, he backed his horse until the wagon started to move.

"Hold on," said Ryan. "I think I can get her out."

Tom stopped the horse, and Ryan pulled Annie out.

"Okay, let it down slowly," Ryan said.

Tom loosened the rope and the wagon fell down. He dismounted and ran over to his father and Annie.

"How bad is she, Pa?"

"From what I can see, that's a bad break on her left leg. The bone is sticking right out. Have to stop that bleeding. She's also got a bad gash on her head. Let's get her in the wagon and get her into town to have the doc look at her. Round up those horses, and let's get them hitched to the wagon."

They place Annie in the wagon gently and tried to make her comfortable.

"Get back to the house," Ryan told Tom. "Tell your ma what happened. I'm taking Annie into town. You and her can meet me there."

"We'll be there as soon as we can, Pa."

Tom rode off, and Ryan started toward town, taking it ever so easy, so as not to disturb Annie and her broken leg.

Abby was still waiting on the porch, worrying and praying that all three would be coming up the road shortly, but nobody was appearing.

After a while, she saw a rider approaching the house at full gallop. Abby held on to the pillars of the porch as she watched Tom approaching.

"Mama, there's been an accident."

"Annie?"

"Pa's taking her into town. I came to get you."

"I'll change my clothes."

"I'll saddle you a horse, Mama."

Ryan arrived in town, and the first person to see him was Father Cahill.

"What happened?" he asked Ryan.

"An accident." Ryan spoke quickly. "Father, I don't know much about how it happened or what happened. We came out looking for her and found her pinned under the wagon. I have to get her to the doctor. Forgive me, Father."

He got to Doc Bailey's. Thank goodness, the doc was in.

"Doc Bailey, Doc! I need your help here!"

The doc came out of his office. "Ryan? What happened?" He rushed over to the wagon and saw Annie was still not conscious. "Oh my, how long has she been this way?"

"We found her that way, and the wagon was on top of her."

"Let's get her in the office and see what we have going."

Ryan picked her up and carried her into the office and past the waiting room, right into one of the examining rooms.

The doc started to check Annie. "Ryan, I want you to stay outside, I'll let you know what I find."

He left the room as Abby rushed into the office.

She ran to Ryan first. "Annie?"

"The doc is with her now. He'll let us know what happened to her and how bad it is." He wrapped his arms around her.

"Oh Ryan, why? Why my Annie?"

Ryan tried to calm her down. "She's strong, and the doc will let us know as soon as he's done." Ryan helped her to one of the nearby chairs, and Tom sat beside them.

The door opened, and they all looked up. Father Cahill came in. "I thought I'd come to see how Annie was doing."

"Nothing yet, Father," Ryan said, "but if you could say a word to the man upstairs, I'd appreciate it."

The priest silently said a prayer for the sweet young girl's recovery.

In the other room, Doc Bailey set her badly broken leg. It was a bad break, in three places. Her shoulder was dislocated, and her head had a bad gash. Slowly, Annie began to moan. Then she loudly cried in pain.

Upon hearing the cry, Abby rushed into the room. "Annie!"

Doc Bailey turned around to look at Abby then at the door. "Ryan, keep her in the other room. I'll call you when she can come in."

Ryan slowly backed Abby out of the room. The waiting was unbearable.

"She's awake, but I gave her something for the pain. She's got a broken leg, three broken ribs, a dislocated shoulder, and a large gash on the head, which caused her to be unconscious."

"Doc Bailey, what caused this?"

"Abby, I can only tell you what happened, not how it happened."

"You're right, Doc, I'm sorry."

He patted her shoulder. "It's all right, Abby. I wish I could tell you more."

241

Tom looked at his older sister. She looked so peaceful, but he wondered how that could've happened to her. Annie knew how to drive a wagon, and with the accident having happened so close to town, Abby found it strange no one else saw it before they did.

Abby moved closer to Annie and gently touched her cheek. "Annie, Mama's here."

Annie opened her eyes. "Mama, oh Mama, it hurts so bad."

"I know, sweetheart, but you're gonna be all right. Now just go back to sleep. Doc Bailey says we can take you home."

Annie tried to smile, but the sedative was starting to take effect, and she fell asleep. Abby looked at the doc with concern.

"She's sleeping, Abby. It's all right," he said.

"When can we take her home?" Ryan asked.

"Well, I wouldn't want to move her for twenty-four hours, but since I know Abby won't leave without her, if you and Tom can get her in the wagon without jiggling her and drive slowly, you can take her home now. Mind you, I will be there in the morning to check on her condition. Also, I'll give Abby some laudanum for the pain."

Abby kissed doc's cheek. "Thank you, Doc. God bless you."

Doc looked at the good father. "I think you're handling that department, right *Padre*?"

Father Cahill smiled and nodded, thankful that his prayers had been answered.

As they walked out of the room, Abby told Ryan, "I won't rest until we get her back home."

"We'll get her home. Don't worry." He turned to Father Cahill. "Father, do you think you could stay with Abby for a little while? Tom and I have to get the wagon ready for Annie to be comfortable in it."

"I'd be happy to stay with Abby. Take your time. We'll be fine."

Tom and Ryan headed out the door to the wagon. They noticed Jack Cahill riding in. Tom remembered that he had been at the farm earlier looking for Annie.

"Pa, that nephew of Father Cahill was at the ranch earlier today, asking for Annie. Seems strange he's riding back into town now."

"Well, he could have stopped off somewhere."

"He doesn't know anyone in town."

Ryan turned around and looked at Tom, then he shook his head. What were they both thinking? Jack was the father's nephew, a simple history professor. He concentrated on getting the wagon ready to take Annie home. While he was padding the sides of the wagon, Tom noticed a bullet in the side of the wood.

"Pa, I don't think Annie's accident was her fault."

He took out his knife and removed the bullet. He held it up to his father.

"Looks like one from a Winchester. Somebody was shooting at Annie. That's why she must have lost control of the wagon and toppled over."

Ryan looked at the bullet. "Don't mention this to your ma. Well, not just yet, that is."

"I understand, Pa," Tom said.

They went back inside to get Annie for the ride.

Father Cahill watched them place Annie in the wagon and blessed them for a safe journey home. Abby sat in the back beside Annie, holding her hand to let her know she was near. She smiled at the good father and thanked him for the blessing.

He patted her hand in return. "Bless you, Abby. Bless all of you."

Ryan started the wagon slowly, and Tom followed behind them with Ryan and Abby's horses.

Father Cahill walked into his house and saw Jack sitting at the table, having a cup of coffee.

"Oh Jack, I was wondering where you were all morning."

"I just went out. I thought I'd take a nice ride and enjoy the day."

"Annie Lochlan had a terrible accident on her way home from town. Seemed her wagon overturned, and she's badly injured."

Jack's facial expression didn't change, as if he hadn't heard a word his uncle said. He just looked at his uncle then said, "That's terrible. Just outside of town, you say?" He shook his head, but he still didn't show the expression his uncle was expecting.

"Yes, well they're taking her back to the farm. Abby feels she could rest better in her own bed. You know how mothers are."

"Oh, indeed I do. By the way, Uncle Edward, I will be going back to Cambridge on the morning train."

"But I thought you were going to spend a week here. You wanted to do some research. Downstairs, I have the books you are looking for."

"I know, but well, I have a few students I had promised to tutor, and well, I can't have them failing my course, can I?"

"No, I suppose not. If you like, you could take the books with you and return them on your next visit."

"That would be fine, Uncle. If you don't mind, I would like to rest a bit before supper."

"Of course."

Jack made his way to his room and closed the door. Jack walked over to the bed and sat down, trying to remain composed.

He couldn't react to the news about Annie because he'd seen it happen. He had been riding on the smaller trail that paralleled the main road when he saw a wagon speeding down the road. He looked up, and from the ridge, two men were firing at the wagon. He got off his horse and slid out of view. He watched as something caused the wagon to topple over and the horses to break free. Terrified, he watched and saw no movement.

He stayed frozen until he was sure they had gone, and he slowly crawled out, making his way away from the accident and took the longer way back to town. That way, he avoided anyone on the main trail. He blamed himself for being a coward and wished he had helped Annie. He had to leave town and go back home, back to the hallowed halls where a coward could hide and never be found.

But Annie, oh dear Lord, she could have died because he was a coward. To tell anyone now would be showing he was a coward and a disgrace to his family.

Back at the farm, Tom and Ryan gently took Annie out of the wagon. Abby ran ahead and opened the door.

"Just put her in the downstairs bedroom. It'll be easier."

Abby turned down the bed and slowly removed Annie's clothes after the boys left. Annie stirred only once. Abby knew she was still in pain. Throughout the night, Annie moaned, which would wake Abby, who stayed beside her.

Early the next morning, Doc Bailey was there as he had promised, to check on his patient.

He knocked on the door, and Abby greeted him. "Morning, Doc. Can I offer you a cup of coffee?"

"First, I'd like to see the patient."

"Right down at the end of the hall."

He walked down the hall and was met at the door by Ryan.

"Morning, Doc."

"Good morning, Ryan."

Doc Bailey walked into the room and saw Annie still sleeping. He took her hand and checked for a pulse. Satisfied with that, he checked her heart.

Abby came and told him, "She was up a few times during the night. I only gave her the laudanum once. I don't know how much pain she is in, but there seems to be discomfort."

"I can tell you she does have more than discomfort, but she's a tough one. Reminds me of her mother." He gave her a smile.

There was another knock on the door, and Abby excused herself and headed down the hall to the front door. Abby opened it, and Father Cahill was standing there.

"Father, good morning. Please come in."

"I wanted to talk to Ryan if I may, Abby. But first, how is Annie?"

"Doc is in with her now. Please come in and sit down. Ryan is in the kitchen."

"Thank you."

He made his way toward the kitchen, where Ryan was with Tom. Ryan offered him a cup of coffee.

"Thank you, Ryan. I have to talk to you."

"Well, I'm right here, Father. Do you need something?" Ryan poured him a cup of coffee and placed it before him.

"I have some information on what happened to Annie."

"You know who did this, Father?" Tom exclaimed. "Who did this to my sister?"

"That I don't know. I do know that it was two men who were shooting from the ridge on the main road from town."

"And how do you know this, Father?" Ryan asked.

"I cannot give my source. There is the sanctity of the confessional, and I cannot tell my source."

"Is this source trustworthy?"

"Very trustworthy."

"Well, Father, make yourself at home. Tom, tell your mother I had to go run a little errand."

"Did I help?" Father asked.

"Father, you helped save Annie. Let's hope they never get the chance to hurt her again."

Tom and Ryan didn't take long to find the spot the priest had been talking about.

Ryan looked around the ridge. It was a perfect place for an ambush. For some reason, Ryan felt throughout the experience he and Tom should go back to the house. Something kept telling him to get back.

Abby was sitting in the kitchen with the good father when she heard sounds outside. She listened again and moved quietly to the door.

As the back door was slowly opening, Abby grabbed a vase and was ready to smash it on the intruder's head. Suddenly, she heard a familiar voice.

"Mama? Mama, is everything okay?"

"Daniel, what are you doing here?"

"I was in town, and they said Annie was in some sort of accident."

"As far as we know, she was on her way home from town, and she lost control of the wagon. It tipped and pinned her under it."

"How is she now?"

"She's pretty banged up. You can go see her if you like."

Daniel headed to the stairs, and Abby called to him, "She's in the downstairs bedroom, Daniel."

There was movement on the top of the ridge on the other side of the road. Abby couldn't say who it was, but they had been there for a while. Suddenly, Tom and Ryan turned onto the road leading to the house. Abby looked at the ridge again, but it was clear. No one was up there.

Across the road at the bottom of the ridge, three men were inside a cave, waiting. The cave was dark, and their faces couldn't be seen. The only thing that was clear was that they were from New England.

"Look, you two got sloppy today. There was to be no mistakes, and I find you running the wrong woman off the road."

"You told us it didn't matter which one."

"I suggest you both get out of this part of the country and don't show your faces again."

"Hey, I've got a question. What did this woman do to you?"

"It's none of your business."

# CHAPTER TWENTY SEVEN

Ryan and Tom went home and found Abby sitting in the kitchen.

"I was wondering where you were," she said.

"Is everything all right?" Ryan asked. "I had this feeling that I had to get home."

"No. Everything is all right. Daniel is in there with Annie, and Father Cahill left a moment ago."

He looked at his wife closely and knew she was holding something back.

"Are you keeping something from me? I suggest you don't. I don't want to see another incident."

Two months passed after Annie's accident, and her recovery was still progressing. She enjoyed her afternoon walks around the yard and sitting on the porch to watch the sunset. Although she appeared to be happy, in her dreams at night, she would relive that day over and over again. At times, she cried out in her sleep. Those were the times Abby would hold her until the fear subsided and she would sleep once again.

Doc Bailey had suggested she take a trip to get a change of scenery that would help her. Though her sisters offered to let her visit them, Annie refused, saying she was happy at the farm.

Abby feared Annie would crawl into a shell as her Aunt Mary had done years before. This troubling thought motivated her to send a wire asking Mary and Mick to come for a visit.

As she sat at the kitchen table, she smiled, reading the wire they'd sent back, saying they would be on the first train leaving for Boston the next day. This was the answer to her prayers. She wanted so much to see if Mary or Mick could help Annie. Mick especially was always so wonderful at cheering others up.

She was making breakfast when Ryan came in.

"Morning, Abby."

"Morning. What would you like?"

"Only coffee, please. I promised Daniel I'd go with him to pick out some new stock at the stock show. He was looking at a fine bull yesterday and wanted my opinion on it."

"All right. By the way, Mary and Mick are coming for a visit. They'll be here in three days."

"Mick got time off from work? Is there anything wrong?"

"No. They wanted to come to see how Annie was doing. And Mary thinks I could use some help."

He took her in his arms and held her close, as he was fond of doing. "I know it hasn't been easy for you these past months. It's hard enough dealing with the farm and all, but since Annie isn't well, you've taken the whole burden on yourself, and I... well, I should have helped more."

She knew he was trying to apologize, but she was more than worn out.

"I know you've been busy with the farm, and after all it's my fault."

He tried to hold her closer, but she backed away.

"I have to see if Annie's up. She may want breakfast. I'll see you when you get back."

She walked out of the kitchen, leaving Ryan wondering, *Where is the girl I know, who is so strong?*

Tom came into the kitchen after seeing his mother enter Annie's room. "Is something bothering Mama?"

"I don't think so," Ryan said. "Why?"

"I don't know. She just didn't seem like her usual self."

Ryan thought nothing of it and headed out the door. Tom soon left too.

With everyone else out, only Abby and Annie were in the house.

The shadows of three figures slowly made their way toward the house. Slow and steady, the men inched their way toward the porch like snakes, toward the dining room window.

Abby was in the kitchen, getting Annie's breakfast ready. Silently, the window opened, and one by one, the figures climbed in.

Abby placed the eggs on a plate. "Annie, breakfast is ready."

Suddenly, a feeling came over her. Something was not right. "Annie?"

She raced to the door of the kitchen and opened it to see Annie being held by two of the three men. One of them had a hand over her mouth, muffling her screams.

Abby gasped. "You!"

"Good morning, Mrs. Lochlan."

"Tim McIntire, what are you doing here? Have your men let go of my daughter!"

"Well, you see, Mrs. Lochlan, last time we left here, we had a little unfinished business, and well..."

"If you know what's good for you, you'll get out now!"

He turned to the two men holding Annie. "What'd I tell ya? She's got spunk—always did. I remember the time before we had just left the army. Well, I came here since I was sweet on her sister Mary. I figured it couldn't hurt since her pa left his girls all that money. Who cared what Mary looked like as long as I got my share of the money?"

"Tell your friends to get their hands off my daughter now!" Abby yelled.

Tim only looked at her and smiled. "Still think you're firing orders, don't ya? You just go back in the kitchen and sit down. And just maybe we'll leave you and this pretty little lady alone." Tim noticed the plate of ham and eggs. "That's real nice of you, Mrs. Lochlan, fixing breakfast for me. Tell ya what, my friends would like some, so why don't you make yourself useful and make another two plates." He turned to Annie. "Sorry for the accident a few months back. The two men who had been with me got a bit carried away, and–"

Abby turned, with a knife in her hand, and lunged at Tim. "You bastard! You did this to my daughter. I'll kill you!"

One of his men let go of Annie and grabbed Abby's arm that held the knife.

"Calm yourself, Mrs. Lochlan," Tim said. "I said I was sorry. Besides, she looks fine."

"What do you want?" Abby demanded, exasperated.

He smiled. "*Finally.* We get to the reason for me being here. I know your old man left money to all of you girls. Since I did have feelings for your sister, I figure it was worth fifteen thousand dollars for the time I spent with her, and after all, I did go to war."

"So did others."

"Really? I never heard about your husband going off, and he's got this whole big farm just 'cause he married you."

Abby blinked at him. "You have no idea what you're talking about."

"Don't I? Your husband was a nobody when he came here. He bargained with your pa to get the rights for the railroad to use his road to send their supplies in. A year later, you're his wife. Not bad for a dirt farmer from Ireland. Your sister Jenny, she spent all her money and left her husband, and when she wanted to go back to him, your other sister had already snatched him up."

"Are we going to go through the whole life of the McVinny family? If so, I've heard it before, even lived through it."

Tim put his arm around Annie. "You know, Mama, if you was a bit nicer to me, I might leave your pretty little gal alone. What about that, pretty little gal? Would you like to be left alone or have a good time with me and the boys?"

Without anyone's hand on her to silence her, Annie looked at Tim straight in the eyes and, without blinking, said, "Get your filthy hands off me, and stop slobbering all over me like some rabid dog."

Even Abby was surprised.

"So you have spunk like your mama. I like spunk..."

Annie head-butted the man holding her from behind. Screaming in pain, he let go of her arms so she was free to pull out Tim's gun. She aimed it right at him.

"Now, little girl," Tim said in a warning voice. "You don't want to do something foolish, and that gun might go off."

"Well, you know it just might, Mr. McIntire, and make no mistake. I do know how to use a .45, and I always hit what I aim at. My papa taught me how to shoot, and my grandpa and Uncle Gideon always said, when in doubt, always aim for the gut. Now, you were saying about shooting?"

"I believe, Mr. McIntire, the tables have turned," Abby said.

One of Tim's men started to move toward Abby again when Annie called to him.

"I suggest, if you don't want another belly button, Mr. McIntire, it would be wise to tell your friend to stand very, very still. Never know, I might just shoot you, and we're having such a good time here."

"Morgan, Sills, don't make a move," Tim commanded.

"Hey, she can't get us all," the one named Sills said.

"No, but she'll hit me."

Morgan looked at him. "You afraid of a little girl?"

"When the little girl is holding a .45 aimed at my gut, I am."

"Bet she can't shoot it anyway."

"If you want to see if she can or can't, I'd be happy to let you take my place."

Abby smiled. "It's a bit different, Tim, isn't it, when you're not pulling the strings?"

"Come on, Tim, where's the money you kept saying was here?" Sills said. "I see nothing but an old woman and a girl that's slightly demented."

Tim turned to Morgan with exasperation. "Shut up, or she'll shoot me."

"So your friend thinks I'm demented," Annie said. "It was you three who shot at my wagon that day. You left me there to die, and now you want forgiveness? I don't think so."

She cocked the hammer back and aimed the gun.

"Annie, no!" Abby screamed.

"I'd listen to your mama, Annie," Tim said. "I'm sorry we left you out there, but we thought you were already dead. You have to believe me. I would have gotten help for you if I knew you were alive. I really don't want to get my insides blown to kingdom come."

"I've never seen a person's insides blown to kingdom come," Annie said. "I might consider doing it."

"See, I told you she's demented," Sills said.

# CHAPTER TWENTY EIGHT

Tom Lochlan had turned around and come back to the house. He'd heard a woman's voice calling out to him and had slowed his horse, turning around to see the open window from the hill. That window was never open. He knew he had to be cautious, and he carefully tied the horse to a tree and walked the rest of the way back to the house.

He noticed no other horses around. His mother and sister were nowhere in sight. Slowly, he unholstered his Colt and went through the window.

He heard voices in the kitchen. His mother's and Annie's, he recognized. It was the other three he didn't. As he looked through the crack of the kitchen door, he saw Annie with a gun on one of them and the other two just standing there. He realized Annie with a loaded gun was not a good thing. If he were to burst in right then, she could easily shoot him, the man sitting, or even their ma. He needed a better plan.

As Ryan and Dan were coming home from town, they were stopped by a posse headed by a lawman named Quint Lockheart. Ryan had met him years before when he worked for the railroad.

As Quint approached, Ryan stopped the wagon. "Hi there, Quint. What takes you this way, and why all the extra guns?"

"Ryan Lochlan, dang it's been a long time. It must've been twenty years or more."

"Or more, Quint. Still wearing the badge?"

"Marshal now."

"I'm impressed. Say, what brings you to Fall River, and why all the guns?"

"Well, we've been after three prisoners who escaped a prison wagon over a month ago."

"You think they'd be here?"

"Seems one of them hails from round here. Name's McIntire, Tim McIntire. Do you know him?"

Ryan's face turned white as he looked at the marshal. "I know him all right, and if he's around here, he may try to get to my farm. We got to get there, Quint. The only ones there are Abby and my daughter Annie."

"Lead the way, Ryan."

They came in through the back way, leaving the horses down the road.

Nobody seemed to be around, and Ryan didn't like the sight of that. "Quint, I want your promise you'll let me go in and see that Abby and Annie are safe from fire."

"All right. I'll give you that, but no more than five minutes, and we'll be coming in both doors."

Ryan climbed up the large maple tree on the side of the house. He made it to the second porch and in through the bedroom window. Once inside the house, he quickly made his way down the stairs.

He saw Tom against the wall outside the kitchen. He tugged at the rug under Tom's feet, making him look up.

Slowly, Tom made his way to his father. "They're in the kitchen."

"How many are they?"

"Three, and Annie's got a gun on one of them."

"Where did she get a gun? Never mind. She's your mother's daughter. Well, there's a whole posse outside waiting to storm in here, and we've got to get Annie and your ma to safety."

"We could kick in the door, the other two would fall, and hopefully, Annie won't shoot us."

"It looks like the only chance we have. Are ya ready?"

They moved toward the kitchen, and on a quiet count of three, they burst through the door and knocked Morgan and Sills into Tim. They knocked into Annie, and the gun fired and hit the ceiling.

Abby ran to her daughter to get her out of the way just as the marshal and his men came charging in. With very little gunfire, the posse overpowered the prisoners before they had time to fire a shot. Ryan ran to his wife and daughter to make sure they were all right.

The frightening experience was over before it started. The marshal and his posse were ready to leave with their prisoners.

Abby, as always, graciously thanked them. "Marshal Lockheart, if you are ever in this area again, I would be honored and proud if you would stop and have supper with us."

"It was a pleasure meeting you, Mrs. Lochlan, and your family. Ryan is a very lucky man."

"Why, thank you ever so, Marshal."

He tipped his hat to her and Annie. "Ladies." With that, he rode down the road and back home.

Ryan looked at Annie. "Didn't we always tell you not to touch guns?"

Abby interrupted, "Ryan, didn't you teach her how to shoot?"

"No, she's terrible with a gun. She's afraid to pull the trigger."

Shocked, Abby turned to Annie, who was smiling and said, "*They* didn't know."

"You mean you lied about it all?"

"I'm good at it. I learned from Grandpa. He had so many good ones he pulled off, and no one knew."

"Annie Lochlan, I don't ever want to see or hear you do something like this again. You could have been killed. If those men knew–"

"But they didn't know," Ryan said, "and that's what gave you that extra time for help to get here."

Life went back to normal, just in time for the arrival of Mary and Mick. Maryanne and Peyton were in school and could not come that time, but Annie loved having Mary and Mick all to themselves. Of course, Ryan had to tell them about Annie and her bluff with the gun.

"It has to be a McVinny trait," Mick said, smiling. "Your grandfather threatens your father with an empty shotgun, Abby does the same thing, and now Annie, who doesn't even know how to fire a gun, holds off three prisoners until help arrives. It's unbelievable."

"Oh, how you do go on," Mary said. "Our papa didn't think it necessary for ladies to use a gun."

"Ladies?" Mick said. "Mary, I love you dearly, but I would not think of you or Abby as ladies."

"I beg your pardon?"

"You can beg anything you like, my love, but I don't see you as a lady. You and Abby are not the selfish, conceited grand ladies that are all over Washington. You, my sweet girls, are and always will be our fair maidens, who we will love, fight for, and protect all of our days."

A knock came from the front door. It turned out to be the rest of the family, wanting to come in. Someone had heard that Annie was better, and her sisters wanted to come and see her.

Mick and Mary had cooked up the surprise, and no one was supposed to tell until they all met at the train station in Boston.

Abby was truly surprised. She had not been prepared at all. The house was filled with music and laughter again, and so many memories were brought back as each of them recounted stories. Grandkids ran around the backyard, singing songs they had heard growing up.

Abby and Molly told them about gypsies dancing in the moonlight and how they played bagpipes. They told them about a land far across the ocean called Galicia, where the Celts had first settled before they went to Ireland.

After everyone had gone to sleep, Abby and Ryan sat on the back porch and watched the night sky. A shooting star raced by, and then another.

"Ryan, look! Quick, make a wish."

He smiled at her. "I don't have to. I have all I want and need."

"Is this really what you wished for? I mean, did you find your dream?"

He looked into those warm eyes of hers that he never got tired of. "I did have a dream. It was the only thing that kept me going those lonely, long two months on the ship. It was the only thing that made me take the job on the railroad instead of staying in Boston. I often wondered when I would find this dream and how would I know it when I saw it. And then I saw you—you with those eyes that seemed to look straight into my soul and haunt me with a sweet memory of a love I never felt before. You captured the dream I wanted, and I knew that you would be a part of my dream and life for the rest of my days. I was right."

"Do you ever wish we could just turn back time and bring back those we loved for just a day?"

"All the time, Abby. I miss them all so much and only wish my parents had seen their children and grandchildren. It would have made them so proud."

In Ryan, Abby saw a wonderful man—her man. Her mother had been right.

She wondered what was next for their family.

What will the next generation of Lochlan-McVinny grandchildren bring? Will there be a congressman, a senator, maybe a president? Would Abby and Ryan's legacy bring not only honor to the family but to the country? The country was growing each day, and new settlers were constantly arriving to find their dreams, to follow that rainbow to the other side, to find that pot of gold.

Their grandchildren would be the new generation to move ahead with progress and determination to build those cities, to carve new trails for others to follow, and bring civilization to all parts of the nation, to help the nation heal from its wounds and become united and stronger than before.

Beyond the backyard, on that small hill under the maple tree, the McVinny family rested. Abby faithfully went there each Sunday to spend some time with those she loved.

The only one who dared to venture from her resting place was Molly. She had always been there for her girls and had at times given them a gentle shove. She was so proud of them and their children, but Abby, dear Abby, had taken over Molly's job, to push their family ahead even further. Her gentle smile was a beacon to many. No stranger was ever turned away, and no stranger ever stayed a stranger for long.

Molly loved both her sons-in-law, but she loved Ryan more. Maybe the reason was that he had made Little Annie feel so special. Annie had loved him as much as a fourteen-year-old could understand love. That's why he and Abby had given birth to Annie, his daughter. Abby was only going to have twins, but Molly wanted him to have the Annie they'd lost that day.

Her Mary had been very lonely after her sister was taken from her, and when Mick lost Jenny, not once but twice, Molly gently pushed these two broken souls together and made them not only whole but a family.

She watched as Ryan cradled Abby in his arms. Their love was unlike any she had ever known, and that was how she knew they were one soul.

When she was alive, she had tried to teach her girls about the spiritual side of their souls, but it had been hard to explain to them, and it would be still, especially now. But she knew Abby and Mary saw her and, at times, could even hear her voice. She was so proud of her girls and her entire family. Theirs was a family who believed in truth and honesty and was brave and loving and generous. Each generation passed on gifts for the coming generations, and she was sure those gifts would carry on.

Molly felt the love in the room as she continued to watch Ryan and Abby in their moment of peace. Nothing was better than knowing that her family was well and happy.

# About the Author

Chloe Emile writes sweet, clean romance, whether it's contemporary or historical. She can usually be found working on her next novel, eating takeout with her husband, or watching rom-coms.

Visit Chloe's website for the latest updates.

**www. ChloeEmile.com**

Chloe Emile